MICHAEL McLAVERTY

Call my brother back

Edited with an introduction by
SOPHIA HILLAN

THE
BLACKSTAFF
PRESS

BELFAST

First published in 1939 by
Longmans Green

This edition published in 2003 by
Blackstaff Press Limited
4c Heron Wharf, Sydenham Business Park
Belfast BT3 9LE, Northern Ireland
with the assistance of
the Arts Council of Northern Ireland

Typeset by Techniset Typesetters, Newton-le-Willows, Merseyside

Printed in Great Britain by Cox & Wyman

A CIP catalogue record for this book
is available from the British Library

ISBN 0-85640-746-1

www.blackstaffpress.com

To
Michael's grandchildren
and great-grandchildren

ACKNOWLEDGEMENTS

Thanks to Sophia Hillan, joint literary executor, for her careful editing and continuing enthusiasm for Michael McLaverty's literary works; and to the team at Blackstaff Press for their prescience and energy in publishing this new edition.

MAURA CREGAN
LITERARY EXECUTOR

INTRODUCTION

First published in 1939 to great critical acclaim, Michael McLaverty's *Call My Brother Back* is acknowledged as a classic of Irish literature. By the time the novel was written, McLaverty was already a respected writer of short stories and had been published in a number of prestigious journals and literary magazines. In spite of this success, however, he had had to acknowledge that publishers did not want the short story, regarding it as too much of a commercial risk. Encouraged, deflected even, into the novel form, he embarked on *Call My Brother Back*, a poignant and beautiful elegy set in the 1920s, following the fortunes of thirteen-year-old Colm MacNeill and his family as they are forced to leave their island home on Rathlin and make a new life for themselves in Belfast. Like the short stories that preceded it, the novel is deeply concerned with the plight of the innocent and the dispossessed in a world of hard experience. It was an immediate success and McLaverty was praised in particular for his sensitive evocation of landscape and his lyrical fusion of place, mood and character. His writing was compared to that of James Joyce, Patrick Kavanagh, Frank O'Connor and Sean O'Faolain.

The novel developed out of two short stories written by McLaverty some years earlier. The first, 'Pigeons', about a small boy on Belfast's Falls Road whose brother, an IRA man, is shot dead, was published in the April/May 1936 edition of *New Stories*, edited by Edward J. O'Brien. From 'Pigeons', the child's deep love for his older brother, his grief at his loss, and his pragmatic determination to keep going at the end of the story are carried into *Call My Brother Back*, as is the scrupulously plain and unaffected style of writing. The second story upon which the novel was built was the 1937 'Leavetaking', about a boy leaving Rathlin for school in Belfast. In many ways 'Pigeons' was the more important of the stories. Not only was it beautifully crafted, but its publication brought McLaverty into contact with Edward O'Brien, the same who encouraged Ernest Hemingway when all but one of his manuscripts were lost on a train. A mentor to McLaverty as to Hemingway, O'Brien was also responsible for introducing McLaverty to the American publishing company Longmans Green, who accepted a novel that McLaverty submitted under the title *Waste Ground*, and published it as *Call My Brother Back*.

The novel is deeply rooted in McLaverty's own childhood experience. He spent early childhood holidays on Rathlin and, growing up during the same troubled times as Colm in Belfast, made the same hazardous journey every morning to St Malachy's College, the model for St Kevin's. In an account given by McLaverty in 1947 to Matthew Hoehn for his *Catholic Authors*, the inspiration for the novel is given:

> His first novel ... came to him on a visit to Rathlin,
> and in an old house overlooking a lake he discovered
> an account of the 1935 Belfast pogrom. As he read it,

all the twisted life of that city, which he had experienced as a boy, suddenly surged with compulsive force into his mind, and seeing a few swans in the lake below him he thought of Yeats's beautiful poem, 'The Wild Swans at Coole'. The recollection of this poem re-illuminated for him the tranquility of the island life compared with the pitiable waste of blood that was spilt in the poorer quarters of Belfast.

Without doubt, McLaverty may be said to be at his best in the Rathlin section of the novel, and in moments of inscape such as the lonely Colm's homesickness for Rathlin, where the playful desperation of a prisoner waving to him from the Crumlin Road gaol is delicately suggested in the image of a handkerchief as a captured seagull. In his vivid recollections of his school, and of the violence of the city, McLaverty writes from experience, paying homage to his acknowledged master, James Joyce. He recreates vividly the summer of 1921, when 'peace came to the city and hovered over it like a spring cloud'. In this brief time of respite, the three MacNeill brothers climb to the top of Belfast's Whiterock Road and look down at the city and the countryside beyond. What most takes their imagination is the great number of churches and the generally unsympathetic Alec shows a rare and wry humour in his rhetorical question: 'Wouldn't you think now to see all the churches . . . and all the factories and playgrounds that it was a Christian town?' Shortly afterwards, when Alec is shot, McLaverty makes his own comment on the futility of sectarian politics through a street orator in Belfast's Royal Avenue:

Supposin' ye got all the Orange sashes and all the Green sashes in this town and ye tied them around loaves of bread and flung them over Queen's Bridge,

> what would happen? What would happen? The
> gulls – the gulls that fly in the air, what would they
> do? They'd go for the bread! But *you* – the other
> Gulls – would go for the sashes every time!

At the end of the novel, all passion spent, McLaverty speaks
in quiet and restraint, recalling the delicate harmony so
characteristic of the early stories. Colm, one brother dead,
the other gone to England, takes a lonely journey by tram
to the end of the lines. There, in open country, 'all this
beauty, all these quiet places flowed into his heart and filled
him with a tired-torn joy'. It is perhaps that Hopkins-like
phrase, 'a tired-torn joy', wrung from the exhausted Colm
as he begins life once again, which most speaks to
McLaverty's feeling for what Patrick Kavanagh called
'important places'. McLaverty was frequently exasperated
by the places he loved and the people who lived in them,
but kept faith in humanity and in the resilience of the
human spirit, its endless ability to renew itself through the
redemptive power of natural beauty. *Call My Brother Back*
carries his passionate frustration and his stubbornly
resurgent hope in the possibility of a better future. This may
be one reason why Seamus Heaney has described the novel as
'among the verifying texts of modern Ulster writing'.
McLaverty himself felt less confident about the redeeming
power of the novel and was reluctant to have it reprinted in
the late sixties, lest it stir up old hatreds. There was no danger
of that, any more than there was substance to his anxiety that
the last chapter in the first section, where he describes the
looting of a ship wrecked off Rathlin, would prejudice
readers against the islanders who were his early friends.

Call My Brother Back is, it must be said, an uneven novel.
While the Rathlin section expands naturally into an
evocation of the lost Eden of childhood, the Belfast chapters
of the novel are at once more difficult and more intriguing.

The recollection of turbulently conflicting emotions makes for a passionate picaresque, sometimes disturbing in its hurtling haste, as though the writer could not wait to set down all that he recalled. McLaverty's projected title, *Waste Ground*, carries much of his anger and frustration at the violence and sectarianism of Belfast as well as suggesting Colm's bitter weariness at the end of the novel. The evocative title *Call My Brother Back*, suggested by Longmans Green and accepted by the author, is more reflective of the human element of the novel and of the sense of longing and loss that is so much a part its final mood. McLaverty's great triumph is that he manages to produce this lyrical evocation of character and place and still remain true to the hard political realities of his time.

SOPHIA HILLAN

AUGUST 2003

BOOK ONE

THE ISLAND

'They paddle in the cold
Companionable streams . . .'

W.B. YEATS
'The Wild Swans at Coole'

ONE

A dark cloud with tattered edges came drifting over the shoulder of the island scattering grains of rain upon the rocky land. From the slope of a hill a small boy watched the cloud approach. Nearer it came, the wind hurrying it along. The boy ran to the lee of the hill and snuggled into a cleft of rock. Around it the earth had been trodden bare, and, yesterday, on the rock-face he had carved his name:

COLM MacNEILL, 1918
AGE 13

His little body trembled slightly when he saw the land darkening and shrivelling as if the very cracks in the earth were tightening against the oncoming rain. Below him was the sea squall – streaked and dark, the gannets striking into it and the water breaking white where they met the surface.

A few heavy drops spattered coldly on his bare legs, and he shifted his position, tucked his feet under him, and

gathered up the lapels of his coat. He felt warm in his new
position as he peered at the rods of rain jagging into the
grassy patch beside him. It fell for a long time, bending the
grass and filling the rocks with little pools. He would have a
great time when the rain stopped, stamping his bare feet in
the rock-pools and scooping the water away with his hands.
A few wind-blown drops thubbed on his cap and he
gathered himself up like a snail in its shell.

In front of him a gull was flying into the wind and rain,
banking and dipping, but never turning. And sitting
huddled and sheltered Colm let his thoughts wander to it
... Poor lonely bird! The rain will get into its yellow eyes;
its wing feathers, blue and smooth as a beach stone, will
ruffle with wet. In their holes in the sand the puffins are
warm, the rain won't get near them. The spiders that live in
the rock-cracks will gather up their legs for fear of it; the
cruel rain will tear their webs. The stones and leaves will let
it slide over them. The beasts in the fields will stand against it;
and the hens will hunch their backs and shake it from them!
... A trickle of cold rain dribbled down his neck and
banished his thoughts in a shiver. He drew in his breath
with a hiss and rose to his feet.

The cloud was now drifting towards the Mull of Kintyre;
to the right an arc of a rainbow hugged the land, its curve
increasing as the rain thinned. The evening sun shook itself
free from its cage of clouds and a whin-gold light winged
slowly across the fields. Suddenly the colours of the
rainbow flamed and burst in liquid brilliance; and looking
at it the boy's heart ached with a sweet, yearning sadness.

He sighed, gave his cap a shake, and put it on with the
peak to the back. At his feet he plucked a blade of grass and
spilled the raindrops from it upon his tongue. He pressed the
blade between his thumbs, blowing with all his might, and
trembled the air with reedy sounds. A slap of bare feet made
him turn with a start.

'What the divil are you doin', Colm, that you haven't the cow yet? Me father's goin' to fish and he's goin' to take us out,' panted Jamesy, his younger brother.

'I was sheltering from the downpour. Come on with me, Jamesy, and we'll both fetch her.'

The two brothers were alike in appearance, fair-haired, blue eager eyes, and tanned faces. Jamesy was thinner, his long bony wrists stretching out from the sleeves of his brown jersey. They scampered down the hill, Colm running across the wettest rocks, and scooping the water from the pools with his feet.

'Ach, come on quick,' shouted Jamesy, watching the shiny belts of water slapping over the rocks.

When they entered the little field they raced to the cow, their bare heels spattering drops from the grass. The cow stood with her forelegs splayed and as the boys ran past her she kicked up her hind legs and raced off with her tail stiffened out behind.

'Now look what you've done,' said Colm. 'You'll turn the milk.'

'It was you done it; you're always getting me to race you, when I'm tired.'

Colm trotted off to where the cow stood with nostrils steaming, and a few rain-tired flies flitting around her head.

'Poor Daisy! Poor Daisy!' he petted. 'What are they doin' on you?' He scratched her on the head and they set off.

Daniel, their father, was leaning against the jamb of the open door and when he heard the boys' voices, he gathered up the boat rods and went to meet them. He was a small man, pared to the bone, and stooped by hard work.

They went down to the shore. The boys trotted in front, jumped over stones and cart-wheeled on level ground.

'There'll be fish in it tonight for I saw the gannets diving off the point,' said Colm.

'I heard me father sayin' it's an evenin' the fry might be in.

He saw a quare lot of gulls when he was burnin' the kelpy rods.'

'Man, we'll have the great sport if they're in.' The road dwindled to a bay of yellow sand. The boys shouted with delight and a flock of gulls all facing windward rose up and settled out at sea. When Colm reached the edge of the tide he saw tracks of the gulls' feet in the sand and little feathers shivering in the wind.

They launched the boat without their father's help.

'You'll soon be able to do without me at all,' he said, when he saw the boat in the water and Colm at the oars.

'Have we to lift the lobster pots?' Colm asked.

'We'll not bother. I put fresh bait in them a wee while ago and we can lift them early in the morning. Head her up towards the lighthouse.'

Colm pulled at the oars and the boat slapped gently out from the sheltered port. It was a lovely evening. A little breeze fidgeted over the sea, but the swell was dying with the ebb. Behind the hills of the island the sun had set, leaving red wounds in the sky. The air was clear, and far off the Kintyre lighthouse was a splash of lime on the Scottish cliffs. The boat kept close to the shore where black rocks nippled by limpets breasted the sea.

Daniel lit his pipe, tucked the tails of his muffler under his oxters and took the oars. Jamesy coughed as the heavy tobacco smoke floated down to him. Colm sat beside him on the stern seat; and quickly they unloosed the lines in silence while the boat moved under the big cliffs of the East Lighthouse. Here it was cold like the air above a spring well. It frightened Colm when he looked at the black-green cliff and listened to the water scowling and rumbling in the caves. But he said nothing to Jamesy. He tried not to look at the cliff, tried to listen to the wooden thumps of the oars or watch the curving flight of puffins making in from the sea, but when the line began to pluck, his fear dissolved in breathless excitement.

Slowly he bent his rod and began hauling the line steadily. 'Oh-o-oh!' he shouted as he felt the heavy tug on the line. 'He's a brute! He's a brute!'

'Take him aisy now, aisy.'

Old Daniel watched the line, now pulling stiffly on the oars, now slackening as the line tautened. Colm stopped hauling and held on; the line was straight down in the water. He stood up in the boat, his wrists throbbing with the strain.

'Hold him, Colm boy! Don't slack,' encouraged the father. 'He'll give in, in a wee minute or two.'

The fish ran out from under the boat, its large white belly turning and its tail threshing a misty trail in the green water. Colm leaned over and began pulling in the line; the fish came easier with it.

'Wait'll I get the gaff: you'll never land him!' shouted the father.

The line loosened; the fish gave a sudden turn and floated to the top; for a moment its gills opened, and Colm leaning out stuck his forefinger into the open gills and lifted the big lithe into the boat. Old Daniel's lips parted as he gazed at the great fish pounding the boards.

'Great man, Colm; he's a clinker!'

Colm looked at the fish, admiring its mushroom-pink gills and the wrack-brown colour of its body. Jamesy sat without speaking, jerking his line now and then to entice the fish. He shifted uneasily as he heard his father's praise and looked anxiously at the line in his hand.

'Now, Jamesy,' the father addressed him, 'don't let Colm get the better of you.'

'Colm always takes the best fly,' he replied without turning round.

'Ah, I think it's the fisherman behind the line,' said the father winking at Colm. Colm smiled. They sat silent.

Then all three raised their heads, listening. Behind the stern of the boat came a fast splutter like gravel thrown in water. Then a patch of water began to patter violently like heavy rain. Mackerel leaped in the air; and then a mad sickle-flash of fish tore the surface of the sea. The boat turned towards the oncoming fry; the lines began to pluck frantically and soon Colm and Jamesy were lifting fish after fish into the boat.

'Shake the fry out of their mouths and put them on your hooks,' ordered Daniel.

They squeezed the herring fry from the gluttonous mouths of the fish and transfixed them to the hooks. The boat drew near the shore where the fish followed their prey in wild fury; the waves washed the fry on to the rocks and their frightened bodies glimmered in the dusk like little knife blades.

When darkness fell, the cliffs gathered black skirts around them. The fish stopped biting and the lines were rolled in. The floor of the boat was a wet-gleaming mass of wriggling fish and now and again some splashed in the water under the stern-sheet.

'That's a brave lump of a fishin', thank God,' said Daniel as they rowed for port, the boys at the oars, each trying to pull the other round. Presently the boat slooshed on the sand and they began to haul her. 'Lift her another wee bit ... Now! ... U–u–up! ... Again! ... That's the men.' They left her on the stones above tide-mark, and then turned to string the fish.

It was very still and dark with the sea licking the rocks, falling with a sad murmur on the sand and receding like an intake of breath.

'I caught sixty-two,' said Jamesy on the road home. 'How many did you catch?'

'I don't know,' replied Colm, 'I didn't count them; it's bad luck.'

'I know how many you caught. Forty-one, not a tail more!'

'Well, if I did, my big one's better than six dozen of your mangey wee things; my arm's near broke carrying him.'

Daniel heard the raised voices and hurried up to them. 'Quit the caperin' or I'll clout the two of you.'

Jamesy turned to him. 'Do you remember the one I caught at Port Gorm last year? Wasn't it as big as Colm's?'

Daniel caught the anxiety in the tone of the voice. 'I was just thinkin' comin' along that they must have been brothers; they're as like one another as two peas.'

'There you are,' said Jamesy to Colm. 'Didn't I tell you mine was as big.'

They walked on quietly with the night-wind shaking a sharp smell from the nettles by the roadside and the dew-wet grass soft and cold under their bare feet. Rover, a cocker spaniel that Colm had got from a lightkeeper, came barking to meet them, and presently they saw the light from the doorway of their cottage.

It was warm in the kitchen with the sods and coal burning red on the raised fire, and the oil-lamp on the wall with a triangle of shadow below it. Bowls with spoons in them were on the table and a pot of stirabout stuttered on the fire. The mother was turning the heel of a sock and near her Clare was dressing a doll.

The boys clustered round the fire and the mother, after great praise for the fish, lifted the pot off the crook, put a white bib on Clare, and handed round the porridge. Colm got the white bowl with the blue rim. He loved to put the warm bowl between his bare knees, fondle it with his hands, and, when finished to pretend the brown cracks inside were a fish-net and to begin counting them. And then he would look up the dark throat of the chimney, at the flakes of shivering soot, and the grey smoke rolling sadly and disappearing through the square at the top. He always looked forward to this time of the evening though it filled him with a strange yearning like that he had experienced looking at the rainbow.

He loved to sit still, to curl into himself, and hold the feeling as long as he could. It came to him from the skit of the daddy-long legs on the lamp as it singed its toes and came to rest on the cool corners of the rafters: from the fire purring in its sleep, from its ruddy glow on Jamesy's face and legs, and from the rattle of the newspaper that Alec sent home every week. And when this feeling deserted him he would fall to thinking of Alec, wondering what he would be doing now in the big city.

Once Alec had sent him a postcard with a bulging three-legged pot on it, and when you lifted the lip off the pot there were twelve little photographs of Belfast folded together like a melodeon: there was one of the shipyards with its gantries: one of Donegall Place with its trams: one of the City Hall with its dome and turrets: and some of Colleges and Castles. Try as he could Colm failed to bring them to life; and tonight when he was wondering what it would be like to ride in a tram or a train Jamesy nudged him out of his dreams.

And then they played at finding things in the fire: goats; a giant with three heads; Colmcille going to Iona in his barque; a house toppling from a cliff. And occasionally for devilment the father squirted a spit in the fire, blotting the things out, till the mother told him he was worse than the children, and that made him stop.

After the rosary, Paddy John Beg came in to hear the news from the paper. He was a small man with a wet moustache, and wore an old paddy hat, both in the house and outside it. His voice was deep; and the moment he seated himself, he would cross his legs, begin grinding plug tobacco between his palms, and Jamesy would clean out the pipe for him with a feather. He was never content until he had the children on the floor to perform for him.

Clare lisped her song in one breath and ran to her mother's lap. Jamesy sang next, preferring to sit where he was in the fire nook for fear Clare would jump in and take his place. Daniel threw him two old boots from below the table, and placing one between his knees with the sole upward Jamesy commenced his song.

> My trade it is-s-s a cobbler,
> A trade I spent all my life,
> And to earn an hon-n-est living,
> I've to work with all-l-l my strife.

And then they all joined in the chorus:

> With your twang, twang, twang twiddle-I
> Twang, twang, twiddle, I-eh,
> With your whack fol-de-diddle I ad-de-day,
> Whack fol-de-diddle I-eh, I-eh.

Jamesy would pretend at the chorus to pull a waxen hemp thread through the sole, and at the word 'whack' he'd wallop the boots together with great gusto. And as the song went on it told how the poor cobbler worked hard, but as fast as he earned the money his wife spent it all in the inn, and how evil befell her in the end.

Then it came Colm's turn and he stood out on the floor and intoned in a loud, clear voice a Latin ode the old island priest made him learn by heart, beginning:

> Vitas hinnuleo me similis,
> quærenti pavidam montibus aviis
>   matrem non sine vano
>   aurarum et siluæ metu . . .

And following quickly he recited its meaning to them –

> Thou dost shun me, like a fawn seeking its timid

mother on the lonely mountains, not without a
groundless fear of the breezes and of the thicket; for
she trembles both in her heart and knees, whether
the brake has rustled with its leaves shaking at the
approach of the wind, or whether the green lizards
have stirred the brambles.

When Colm had finished, Paddy John Beg gave him great
praise, wondering how he could carry all that learning in
his head. Colm looked down at his bare toes and began to
wriggle them. Then a deep friendly silence filled the
kitchen; but when Clare began to sleep on her mother's lap
Daniel sent them all off to bed, and the two men sat closer to
the falling fire, talking and smoking till midnight.

Daniel told of his grandfather that had great Latin verses
in his head, learnt in a school that had no seats, or maps on
the walls, or coloured books like the children have
nowadays. 'There were three schools in the island in his
day; three schools, and now there's only one with forty
wee childer in it.'

'Emigration was the cause of that!' put in Paddy John Beg.
'Look at the many ould wrecks of houses there are strewn
about the place. Nobody spins now and Johnny McQuaid
had to make hen-roosts out of his loom. It bates all that the
land could rear three families in them days where now it can
hardly rear one.'

'The people's not the same as they used to be; there's a
softness in them,' Daniel said quietly.

'We'll soon have nothin' in the island at all only wild goats
and rabbits,' answered Paddy. 'All the young are goin' away,
the ould people are dyin' and there's nobody marryin' . . .
'Tis a pity Colm's goin' from you shortly; that's the third
you'll have away.'

''Deed, God knows it is; but the priest is anxious to send
him to college, he thinks he'll make a teacher out of him. To

tell you the truth, Paddy, I'd rather keep him at home; it'll be lonely for him.'

'Och, with Alec and Theresa near him in the town he'll be all right. Maybe, someday, he'll be back teaching the scholars in the school. Mind you, Daniel, it's an agreeable kind of a job; good hours and brave pay, and a pension to keep the divil from the door in yer ould days. There's few to bate that.'

TWO

Colm's mother shook him gently by the shoulder and he awoke. 'It's time ye were stirrin',' she whispered. 'Get up now for it's a bad wet morning.'

He got up quietly and snuggled the clothes around his sleeping brother. As he dressed he could hear the melancholy drip of water from the eaves and through the window saw the rain falling cheerlessly by the wet-black stones of the potato garden.

In the kitchen it was dark and quiet. His mother was sweeping the floor, the dust yellowing the flames of the fire. She gave him an old coat of his father's to cover him, and for a moment he stood at the door with the coat cowled over his head looking at the heavy rain tinkling into an overflowing jam-pot and lifting the very gravel at the threshold. Under the wet leaves of a thorn bush were the remains of Clare's 'shop': round pieces of clay melting in the rain; blue delft, white delft, and a black shining piece of a broken crock; and in the top-most fork of the bush the rain pelted on a rusty tin he had thrown there a few days ago.

A cold feeling spread over his back and he shivered and ran off. As he slapped along, water swirled in the cart-ruts; the rain-cold air filled with dripping noise; and here and there the puddles stirred in the gusts of wind. A horse stood with its head drooped over the loose wall by the roadside, and near it Colm noticed a frantic movement in the heather. A rabbit with its fur streaked and ruffled was caught in a snare. Colm loosened the wire with difficulty, but when he prodded the rabbit it refused to budge, and he lifted it in his arms and put it under a clump of soaking bracken.

When he came in sight of the chapel he was glad to see no one standing outside in the rain. He had plenty of time. He opened the door and his bare feet left their imprint on the brown linoleum as he padded up the aisle. He waited in the sacristy.

Presently old Malachy Anderson, coughing and breathing heavily, hobnailed into his seat. The priest wasn't down yet, and Colm went up to the parochial house to rap his window. Father Byrne was a bit deaf, and if he didn't hear the alarm-clock his cross housekeeper wouldn't call him. The last time Colm rapped he surprised the priest in his nightshirt, so now he bent cautiously under an angle of the window while his long arm stretched up and tapped the pane. Father Byrne put out his grey head, soap in his ears and a towel in his hands, 'It's all right, Colm, I'll be down right now. Put out the red vestments.'

Colm lit the candles. Soon the priest entered the sacristy rubbing his hands. 'A treacherous morning, an atrocious morning! See they are all in.'

Colm peeped through the slit of the opened door. There were eight or nine scattered on each side of the aisle. He smiled when he saw wee Rosie Doherty; Paddy John Beg had said she was always praying for a man and as many holy medals round her neck as'd anchor a boat. But he missed Nancy Spence. 'We'll give her a few minutes more,' said the priest. 'It's a bad morning for the poor creature to be on the road, maybe she'll not come.'

When Colm looked out again Nancy was there opening the neck of her dolman, and at the end of the seat a tail of rain waggled from her umbrella across the floor.

The ritual of the Mass had no significance for Colm; for him it was a series of mysterious, mechanical movements; its terrifying sacrificial reality escaped him, was not explained to him. But he loved going to Mass; it was Faith. Behind him the few people jingled their beads or fluttered their prayer books. Old Malachy would run a hand through his thin hair, yawn loudly and turn to the beads again; Nancy would lift herself on the seat, half-sitting, half-kneeling, but trying to convince herself and the rest of the congregation that she was kneeling all the time.

As Colm answered the Latin mechanically he thought of the rabbit crouched under the damp bracken, and the cold drops from the fronds falling on the warm sore around its neck. He shivered involuntarily and turned his mind to the Mass again. He rang the bell for the Consecration, seeing a pebble wedged in the broken sole of the priest's shoe and the morning light splintered in gold on the upraised chalice.

Coming from Mass he met Jamesy slithering along the road.

'It's well for you that's left school,' he said, his mouth twisted. Colm smiled.

'Man dear, if he biffs me today for missing my portry I'll brain him, so I will,' he whined, hoisting his schoolbag.

'Wherefore let thy voice rise like a fountain,' mocked Colm. Jamesy made a face at him and paddled off saying aloud to the wet morning:

Wherefore, let thy voice

Rise like a fountain for me night and day
For what are men better than sheep or goats
That nourish a blind man within the brain.

He took out his book, shielding it from the spits of rain. He was wrong again; he'd never get it right. 'That nourish a blind life ... That nourish a blind life ... That nourish a blind life.' He repeated the phrase over and over again. Two wee girls, with a shawl wrapped tightly around the two of them, tittered as they slapped past in their bare feet. But Jamesy's mind was engrossed with his lines and he didn't hear them.

A clump of boys sheltering at the gable-end of the school shouted when they saw him coming: 'Here's MacNeill, boys. Here's MacNeill.'

Jamesy was pleased to see Hairy Dolan in the midst of them.

The master had promised to slash Dolan for mitching. For days he had gone off to the rock-heads with his dog to catch rabbits and to rob sea-birds' nests. He was a big boy with hairs on his upper-lip, fat hands that were black and covered with scratches and finger nails bitten away to stumps. His black hair was cropped to the scalp, his brow was narrow and his face pimply.

He was talking now in his voice that was like a man's. They were all standing around listening intently. Some weeks ago he had come back to the island after an operation for appendicitis, and he had mitched ever since. He lifted up his jersey to show them his wound, and as they looked at the red scar with its ladder of stitch marks, they all noisily drew in their breaths.

Lie after lie he told them about the doctor's knife: how he had sharpened it on a stone bigger than the one at the mill, and how the sparks spluttered from it in all directions. They all listened breathlessly; as their minds leaped and flashed with knives all thought of school was forgotten.

'What was the sewing needle like?' one dared to ask.

'It was as big as that,' he stretched out his arms full length to demonstrate, 'and its eye as big as that in the school key, and when the doctor came to the end of the sewing he pulled tight and bit off the catgut with his teeth.'

'And did you cry?' Jamesy asked.

'A very near, only I scringed my teeth ... The doctor said I was the bravest fella he ever cut up.'

The clanging bell brought their minds back with a jerk and slowly they all trooped into the one-roomed school. Hairy Dolan lagged behind.

When the master saw him in the desk he began to say sarcastically: 'So Mister Dolan has come back to see us at last after long peregrinations. Back to see how we are all getting along ... eh. After a while we'll see how he has been getting along ... eh. And how he has learned his poetry in the free days he has had to himself ... eh.' When Jamesy heard the word poetry he trembled and tried to repeat the lines in his mind, and occasionally cast a fearful glance over at Dolan whose head was bent and face scowling.

The master called the roll and said the morning prayers; then he lifted his poetry book and came over to the seniors.

'Now, Mister Dolan,' he said, fixing his glasses securely on his nose. 'Now, Mister Dolan, "Wherefore let thy voice." '

Dolan held his head down, grunted, and shrugged his shoulders.

'Mister Dolan, we are waiting. Pray don't keep us waiting on such a wet morning. "Wherefore let thy voice" ... Don't know it? Eh.' Down slapped the book on Dolan's head. 'Come out here.'

'No,' gruffed Dolan, still seated.

The master walked to the old harmonium in the corner, lifted the lid, and selected his stoutest cane.

'Hold out your hand like a good boy.'

'Naw.'

The master put his spectacles in his pocket and drew nearer to Dolan with the cane by his side and one hand on his hinch.

'I'm giving you one more chance,' he said tremulously. 'Hold out your hand! ... It is my duty to punish you for truancy.'

There was a dour silence in the room. All eyes were on the master. The colour had gone from his face and the cane twitched in his hand. Dolan kept his head down and refused to budge. He could feel the hot presence of the master coming closer to him.

The master gripped him firmly by the jersey and tried to drag him from the seat. The other boys around him moved to the side. Dolan jerked from the grip and the master fell across the desk and dropped the cane. He lifted it and swished at Dolan with great force. 'I'll tell me da! I'll tell me da,' shouted Dolan.

He came out of the desk and kicked at the master. The cane whistled and the boys stared. A sweet terror flooded them. Dolan fell on the floor and groaned loudly; the master continued to slash at him, and then he stopped suddenly as he saw coming from under Dolan's jersey, red pieces like flesh and kidney. The master gaped: 'God, I've killed him!'

All the children ran out of the school, and Dolan finding the room empty, got up quickly and raced out of the door, over the hills, never turning in his flight.

When the master looked again at the floor he saw the giblets of a rabbit.

'Merciful God,' he breathed. 'Oh, the blackguard,' and he ran to gather in his school.

They all came in, their eyes transfixed with terror. 'Get yer books at once!' he yelled. 'There'll be sore paws before this day's over.' His hands fumbled as he turned the pages of a book. 'There's a lot of blackguards in this island and I'll settle them before very long. I'll settle them!' He banged a desk with the cane and rhymed on. 'I hope you all know your poetry this day. I'll "blind man" some of you before very long.' Jamesy shifted uneasily.

'They say fish is good for the brain – The fool that said that never taught in an island – with your stomachs full of fish and your brains full of blackguardism. I'll keep the whole lot of you in, this day. No one will leave this building until four o'clock.' The children sat still and listened with a respectful fear while their quivering lips hummed their lessons.

A watery sun came out, glittered on the drops of rain on the windows and drenched the room in unnatural brightness. The master breathed loudly through his nose as he looked at the bent heads in front of him. Then outside the large low windows Colm passed and whistled loudly so that the boys would hear him. But no one turned to the windows to regard him; and as he walked by he was conscious of the minds that would follow him, envying him his careless freedom.

Colm turned into the priest's gate and up the white gravel path where his whistling gave way to a shy timidity. He approached the door quietly and peeped through the key-hole, hoping to see the priest standing in the long, oil-clothed hall. He rapped and kept his eye at the key-hole. Then he saw a pair of women's feet coming down the hall. It was the old housekeeper and his heart hammered. He stood back as the door scringed and opened.

'Well!' said the tall, lean woman. 'What d'ye want?' It was the same question every day, the same biting manner.

'Is the priest in?' he answered, his head down.

She looked at him sternly. 'Wait there till I see!'

Colm heard the priest talking. 'Oh, is it Colm? Bring him right on in, Elizabeth; right on in.'

'Here, you; dry them feet!' she said, as Colm stepped into

the hall.

Colm found himself in a small sitting-room where his fear dissolved in the warm glow from the fire and the comfortable presence of the priest. The priest was reading his black breviary, a fringe of coloured ribbons dangling from its gilt edges. He knew to keep quiet until the priest was ready for him.

Far away at the end of the hall he could hear the housekeeper: doors opened and banged; buckets rattled; and now and again she shouted at the hens. But he felt secure in this room with its walls bulging with books and papers littering the green baize table. The air was heavy with tobacco smoke and Colm noticed ashes on the priest's wrinkled waistcoat and matches strewn around the spittoon on the enamelled hearth.

Presently the priest closed his book, rubbed a finger across his eyes, and joined his hands.

'Well, Colm, that's a very necessary job over. And, now, what'll we do today? You haven't long now. Another five weeks, please God, and you'll be sitting at a desk in St Kevin's declining "*Bonus*". You'll be fit to whack the divil out of them all at Latin. Just you learn the beautiful passages by heart, the way I tell you, and someday you'll grow to love the language. Love a language, if you want to learn it well!'

They sat at the table together and the priest read for him, first in Latin and then in English: about wars and seas and boats and deaths. Colm dozed half-way through until some line or lines about rain or sun or wind appealed to him, and he said, 'Father, I like that.'

'You like that, Colm? Beautiful passage! Beautiful language! We'll read it again and then you'll learn it by heart.'

The priest was about to begin when a knock came to the door and the housekeeper came in to say he was wanted on a sick-call. He got up at once, put on his cap with the ear-flaps, gripped his stick, and called to Elizabeth. 'Put more coals on the fire and make Colm a nice warm cup of tea.' Then he turned to Colm, seated nervously at the table. 'Elizabeth will make you nice and comfortable. Learn that passage yourself.'

The door closed and Colm heard with regret the heavy feet crunching on the pebbles. A great stillness came over the house.

Elizabeth entered the room. Colm watched her out of the corner of his eye; she was standing with her hands on her hinches and her lips sucked in.

'Elizabeth'll make you a nice cup of tea! Elizabeth'll do this, that, and the other. Will she, indeed! Don't you think, Colm MacNeill, that I'm goin' to dance attendance on you or any other body on this island. This is the last time I'll make you tea — for two pins I wouldn't make it at all. And furthermore let me tell you, poor Father Byrne's too old to be teachin' the likes of you when he should be restin', poor man.'

Colm didn't speak though at any moment he expected her fist to come down on his back. He was glad when she went out and was sorry to see her back again with tea on a tray.

'The last time I'm goin' to make tea for you. I hope you hear that!' She poked the fire and slammed the door. He was alone again.

On the tray was a cup of tea and a plate with three slices of currant bread. He put two of the slices in his pocket so that he could enjoy eating them in some quiet spot on the hills. He ate the other piece slowly and took a gulp of the warm tea. It was very hot and scalded his mouth. He waited for it to cool, but as he stretched out his arm to lift the Latin book from the table, his elbow hit the cup and it spilled in a steaming mess over the tray. His face flushed as he tried to scoop up the tea with the spoon; then in desperation he wiped the wet slop with the lining of his cap and rubbed it with his sleeve, but the tray frowned back at him.

Elizabeth came down the hall. His face burned. He turned his back to the door and tried to shield the tray. His heart pounded. She planted a bucket in the hall and sighed as she got down on her knees. She began to scrub just outside the door and the loud noise calmed him.

His eyes turned to one of the windows that was open to the air. The curtains swayed gently to and fro. Then the door opened and Elizabeth scrubbed vigorously along the threshold. The door closed again and Colm slipped across the room on his toes, raised the window, and ran off. Near home he stopped, lay flat at a spring well, and took deep draughts of the ice-cold water.

The next morning at Mass Father Byrne never mentioned about the tea and Colm wondered if Elizabeth had told him; yet, he avoided the house for fear of meeting her.

The following Sunday he ran in to her at the corner of the chapel and was surprised to see her in black. Her eyes were red from crying and a handkerchief was bruised in her hand.

In a few broken words he learned that a letter had come with the news that her only sister had died in America. She gave him twopence not to forget the poor thing in his prayers and brought him up to the kitchen where, before a roaring range, she gave him an apple and showered out all her sorrows upon him. Colm put the apple in his pocket and listened uncomfortably to the cries of the woman whom he had feared. Through the window he saw two hens fighting and far beyond them the wind racing like smoke-shadow over a corn field. A sharp smothered cry stiffened the woman beside him.

'Don't cry, Miss King,' he said awkwardly. 'I'm sure she's in Heaven.'

'The poor, poor thing, dying away in America and maybe not a soul there to close her eyes or lift her head ... God protect us all from a lonely and unprovided death.'

After she had wept her fill and talked herself into a sad, tired mood, she let Colm out by the back door and told him again not to forget the poor thing in his prayers.

THREE

'Run down to your Uncle Robert's with the paper. You mightn't get a chance of seeing him before you go away.'

Colm loved to go to his Uncle Robert's. Robert always told him yarns and sometimes Aunt Maggie gave him a farl of warm potato bread with butter oozing across it. He brought Rover with him and went in his bare feet. He had a half-penny for sweets, so he cut down to the right-angular row of slated houses that was the island village, called in the shop, and took the loose stony road along by the sea. Around him walls of limestone hedged the shingly fields, and yellow, wizened rocks stretched long arms into the sea. This part of the island, he often told himself, was white; his own place was grey, because of the rocky hills; and his Uncle Robert's black, because of the lake and the stones that came out of it.

Rover sniffed at a black beetle that was tumbling over the sharp stones on the road; and, bending down, Colm barred its way with a twig, amused to see it climb with its thready legs and then curl itself up, pretending to be dead. He smiled at its cunning, and gently turned it on its back where its thin legs wriggled wildly. 'You're not dead now,' he said aloud, as he prodded it with the twig. Its back was covered with grit and it lay perfectly still. He scooped out a channel in the loose pebbles and left it to escape.

The road climbed gradually out of the village up into the hills where the air was clear and cool. Here he could see Fair Head and dark Knocklayde bulging strangely near. Away beyond that lovely mountain he would be going soon, and as he looked at its cold, rainy folds, he wondered if he would be able to see it from the town.

Standing on a hill facing the road which he had ascended, his eye took in the long, crooked arm of the island; white houses with their backs stuck into the hills; the East Lighthouse like a brooding gull on the cliff-top; and far away over a grey sea a fleet of clouds moored to the wild hills of Scotland. He turned away like one looking on it for the last time, and slowly his head disappeared behind the hill that held in its lap his uncle's cottage.

As he drew near he saw the hens about the open door, a bucket lying on its side, and a brush against the windows. But no smell of baking bread came to him. Maggie was darning a sock and got up when he came in.

'That's a brave day, Colm,' she said. 'Just go on down to the room; Robbie didn't turn a fut the day; the rain in the mornin' scared him.'

Propped up in the bed was Uncle Robert, his forehead seamed with dirt, a woollen shirt on him, and his scapulars round his neck. He was rubbing a hand over his bald head when Colm entered with the paper.

'Och, och, is it you?' he said. 'A'm glad to see you. My pains were that bad I didn't budge the day ... A'm watchin' them thieves of swans that's after comin' to the lake. They'll not leave a pick of feedin' for the ducks.'

Colm looked through the four-paned window at the three swans sailing near the house. One of the swans ducked its neck under the water, its tail in the air waggling, and its black feet almost above the surface. It came up with a green weed dripping from its bill.

'Aw, but that's the thief for you,' said Robert, shaking his fist at it. 'A hould you them buggers are from Scotland.'

Near the swans Robert's ducks paddled amongst the black rocks, and above them on the grass sprawled a grey shirt with its sleeves pegged down with stones. The swans moved towards a little bay which was yellowed with chaff from an emptied bed-tick, and the chaff gathered on their wet feathers as they made tracks in the yellow scum. Colm watched them for a while and then sat on the bed without saying anything.

Robert's woollen shirt was open at the neck and as he bent over the paper there could be seen blue mast-heads of a full-rigged ship tattooed across his chest.

'Is there anything in the paper the day?' he asked, as his cordy arms opened it out. 'D'ye know I can't see a stime without my glasses. Maggie! Where's my glasses?'

Maggie brought him a pair, their legs mended with white twine.

As Robert scanned the paper Colm sat gazing around the familiar room, crammed with old trunks and boxes. Pasted to the bare walls were coloured religious pictures, supplements of Christmas magazines. Trousers hung by their braces from a dinged knob on the bed and under a chair lay Robert's clayey boots with corn-holes cut out in the toes. On the mantelpiece he saw for the hundredth time an old dusty piece of palm leaning like a feather out of a white vase, and, beside it, lying on its side, a green bottle containing a ship in full sail. It was always a puzzle to Colm to know how the ship was got through the neck of the bottle, and every time he asked his uncle, the only replies he got were a fit of laughing and: 'Think it out, boy; it's simple if you think it out.' He was wondering now if his uncle would tell him and he ready to go away from the island in a week's time.

'God, a-god, would you look at that poor craythure,' interrupted Robert, tilting the paper towards him so that he could see the photo of an old Tyrone woman, aged 104.

'If she doesn't die soon she'll turn into a crow,' he added, giving the paper a smack.

Just then Maggie came down to the room with a mug of tea and three pieces of bread balanced on the mouth of it. As Colm chewed the bread she leaned over Robert's shoulder, glancing at the paper and arranging the pillows at his back.

'H'm, there's quare wickedness in the world,' she says, addressing a photograph of Bangor girls in bathing suits. 'Look at them bold heelers and not as much clothes on them as'd dust a flute!'

'Woman, dear,' Robert turned to her sharply. 'Don't meddle with me when I'm readin'; leave me in peace, and I'll send it up to you in a wheen o' minutes.'

'Aw, but that's the cross man for you, Colm. He's as cantankerous as a clockin' hen when he doesn't get the air.'

Colm smiled. They always seemed to be fighting; yet he felt there was a great oneness between them. He recalled an evening not long ago that Robert took the queer wild notion to fish from the rocks by himself. And how Maggie had come up to the house crying and lamenting: 'He'll be killed and drownded this very night. An old man like that with no eyes in his head and no foot under him; he'll slip on them rocks. Go down, Colm, and keep an eye on him.' And later how Robert roared at her when he found her coming to look for him, to help him home, as if he were a drunk man. The recollection brought a smile to Colm's eyes as he sat with the empty tea-mug in his hand and Rover begging up at him for more bread.

'It bates all, the number of words in that paper and nothing in it,' said Robert, closing his glasses. 'A body'd be better keepin' his penny; but, all the same, ye like to get it, afeared ye'd be missin' somethin'. Och, och, but it's queer the notions we have whiles. Alec doesn't forget yez anyway – a fine lump of a fella, Alec! And you'll be soon goin' away from us too. It's sad now to see so many young people leavin' the island and none comin' back.'

From that he drifted into telling about the time he himself left the island, the towns he was in and the boats he stokered to India. And now and again he sat straight up in the bed and bent his arms like a boy showing off his muscles, and shot them out again with great force.

'I was a tight one in me day, a tight fella. And look at me now, Colm, a done man with my blood dryin' up and the dregs of it clogged with grit and dirt ... a body can't get a night's rest with it. God forgive me, but a man'd be better dead when his blood's astray and no comfort in his body. Whiles I think the roof's leakin' when I feel the swirls of air about my head. But it's the blood, Colm, all dried up from stokerin' them bloody boats to Indya. Only for the ould pipe,' lowering his voice now, 'and Maggie, the craythure, I'd be a lonely ould man. Praise be to the good God for pipes. It's heartsome here of an evenin' listenin' to the rain smatterin' on the roof and the ould pipe smokin' like a collier.'

Colm's hand rested on the bed-clothes and old Robert gripped it tightly.

'Whisper, Colm, yer goin' away soon. Listen to me, son; pay heed to an ould battered man. Say yer prayers when yer young; it's then ye love life and if ye give a bit of your time to God 'tis better than givin' a big bit when yer old. D'ye hear me? It's hard to restore an ould limpy ship.'

A scorching sensation came into the boy's throat as he

listened to the quavering voice of the old man, and he turned his head to the window. A wet light was seeping from the sodden sky, shining weakly on the black lake water and whitening the sailing swans.

The hand gripped more tightly his own and he blinked his eyes and gave a nervous little laugh.

'And whisper, Colm, put the heart in the work for if the heart's not there the work's no good ... 'Deed troth, we'll miss you. But as long as Jamesy, the spulpin, is about I'll warrant he'll give us plenty to do.'

They fell silent. A wet sun shone into the room, broke in a thousand pieces upon the lake, and withdrawing its light lost itself in a bundle of clouds. Colm lowered his head and stretched out a hand to the dog who licked it and jumped joyously on to the bed.

'Get down out o' that or ye'll have the place full of fleas,' shouted Robert. 'Maybe now he'd hunt the swans for us. Give him a race at them for we'll have a flood of rain before long.'

Colm and Rover went out. Along the edges of the lake the water was greyed and wrinkled by a little breeze, but the middle reflected the yellow glow of the sky. A wet-gold light dripped from the clouds and a clammy air breathed against his bare legs. The queer light frightened him as he screwed up his eyes to watch scattered gulls flying high and silent. The dog barked and the swans slid out from the edge, breaking the ripples and leaving a smooth trail behind them. He threw a stick into the water and the dog splashed noisily after it.

One of the swans rose heavily, and with loud flaps from their wings and white splashes from the water the others followed. Necks a-strain they circled the lake and as they flew low over the cottage old Robert heard with delight the bing-bing of their powerful wings. Sadly Colm watched them flying northward, while the dog jumped around him barking with joy.

'He done that well; he's a good dog,' said the uncle when they came in again. 'But keep him outside or he'll dreep the place.'

Colm stood in the middle of the floor, his legs apart, and his eyes on the green bottle on the mantelpiece. He lifted it and looked at the schooner inside, turning the bottle with a perplexed look.

'Uncle Robert, are you not going to tell me how you got the ship in the bottle?'

The bed creaked with the laughing. 'Ask yer clever town boyos when you meet them; they'll tell you.'

'Och, go on and tell us!'

Robert laughed the more, and Colm questioned Maggie. ''Deed, child, sure if I knew I'd tell you. I'm thinkin' the ould codger doesn't know himself.'

Robert closed one eye cunningly and stuck out his crinkled tongue at them.

'It's little you have to do but to be tormentin' childer,' said Maggie. 'None of yer nonsense and tell the poor child how to get a ship in a bottle.'

'Are you tryin' to get it out of me, too? It's a secret, woman, a secret! And Robert McCurdy, Rathlin, the County of Antrim, would be known the world over if he let it out. The black niggers of Indya and the yella Chinamen of China would give me a fortune for it. I've sailed and stokered boats the world over. And did I tell my secret?' He points his finger at them. 'NO!' and finished with a loud laugh.

'Good God, would you listen to him, and not as much in his pocket as'd buy an ounce of tobacco.'

Maggie went up to the kitchen, and Robert and Colm sat looking through the window at the sky swirling with ragged clouds and the lake growing mysterious and cold.

'That's a wicked festerin' sky,' put in Robert. 'You'd

better sit and take your ease for there'll be a quare blatter of thunder and a shockin' shower.'

A cold draught flowed into the room. It grew dark and the room cowered. A cheap watch ticked loudly from a nail in the wall and a few scales of rain glistened on the window. Lightning jigged in the house and Maggie rushed into the room and sat on the edge of the bed. She blessed herself as thunder crackled over the scraw of a roof and rain fell battering on the bucket.

Robert turned his back on them and coiled himself up in the bed-clothes, drawing great comfort from the rainy sound.

'Whistle to me when it's over. H'm! Afraid of a spoonful of rain and a chopstick of thunder. Aw, the storms I seen in the Indya Ocean and the rain – monsoons, they called them; ye'd think the ocean was turned upside down.'

Maggie clicked her teeth and shook her head with disdain. She was thinking of the shirt at the edge of the lake and the eggs under the hen in the box; they'd be ruined now, not a bird would be left in one of them.

Colm's eyes were steady with fear as he listened to the brattling thunder. His mind followed a line of swans flying through the rain and beating cold sprays from their wings. Then in a flash he saw the pebble in the priest's shoe; the white stony road passing lonesomely by the drenched cottages; the grit being washed from the beetle's back, and water plaiting itself in the pebbly channel he had made in the road.

The thunder grumbled and barged as it sped over the sea towards Scotland. Sheep bleated from the hills and the lake clopped on the stones.

Colm got up to go and Maggie sent him out for a cabbage leaf as she had some fresh butter for his mother.

The garden was dark with rain and the black soil squelched up between his toes. Shining puddles lay in the furrows and rain freckled the cabbage leaves; when he broke off a leaf it creaked like new leather and the drops rattled off it like pebbles. He stood up and looked north and thought of the swans flying through the wet mists of the mountains and their black feet alighting in the cold waters of a Scottish lough.

It was dusk when he left the cottage, a pair of hand-knit socks for himself in his pocket and the butter snail-cold in the cabbage leaf under his arm. He hurried and went home by the road. The dog panted by his side, and the night-cool air, soft as the touch of a child's balloon, fluttered against his cheek. He splashed in the rain puddles here and there on the road, and all the time his mind kept thinking of the ship in the bottle and his uncle with the gritty blood; but as the thickening darkness hardened the hills and brightened the speckled stars, he became afraid. Rocks and bushes took queer shapes while in front lights glimmered in the scattered homes and the lighthouse revolved spokes of light in the darkness.

He whistled as he passed an empty house, and when rabbits thudded out of danger his heart thumped wildly. Passing by Cnoc-na-Screilan (the hill of the screaming) he blessed himself and ran the rest of the way home. Outside the house he stood to quieten his breathing. The square of light in the window and the noise of his mother talking brought his courage back. Below on the shore the sea grumbled and far off a handful of ships' lights were twinkling. He sighed as he turned into the house.

FOUR

It was the last day of August. The evening sun shone softly into the MacNeill cottage. Clare was putting a shawl round a patient kitten. At the window the mother was giving extra stitches to the buttons on Colm's shirts and putting double buttons on his trousers. Her black hair was combed tightly from the forehead into a coil at the back, and as she bent her head to break the thread the light made shadows on her bony face.

On the window-ledge the geraniums in their paper-covered jampots had been pushed to the side, and the sun sprinkled their shadows on the wall and silvered a spider's web that netted a leaf-space. Her needle caught a line of light as she drew it towards her. Sometimes her hands would rest wearily on her lap as she looked through the window into the potato garden.

Daniel had been digging there since early morning, cutting across the drills horizontally. The turned soil was black and cool under the sun. Colm and Jamesy were kneeling with their backs to the window and they were gathering the spuds. They had taken four drills apiece and were trying to see who would be done first. Beside them were two buckets.

Daniel had moved more than half-way up the field, and now he was digging slowly, thrusting the spade sideways into the drills and toppling the stalks. He was sweating. The hot, sweet smell of the yellowing stalks rose in thick waves, but now and again there came the cool smell of the broken soil to refresh him.

The mother was watching the eagerness of her two boys: Colm slow and careful; Jamesy impetuous, scooping clay and stones along with the potatoes into his bucket. She looked at Daniel stooping slowly and shaking the toppled stalks: she wished he would stop; he had done enough for one day.

He went to his waistcoat that lay on the wall and looked at his watch. He shook his head and smiled at his sons. Then he lifted a lump of clay and threw it at Jamesy; it burst in fragments on his head. The mother laughed; he's as bad as the children. Jamesy raised his head in bewilderment and eyed Colm who was working eagerly. Then he looked at Daniel who leant innocently on his spade. Suddenly realising that he was wasting his time he drew a sleeve across his nose and bent to the work again. Another piece of clay hit him on the back and he jerked his head up angrily. 'Quit the cloddin', Colm: that's the second time you hit me; if you do it again I'll tell me da.'

'Who's cloddin'? You're tired and you want a rest, that's what's up with you.'

For answer Jamesy lifted spuds in each hand and threw them noisily into the bucket. This time the father threw a lump of clay at Colm, and Colm, thinking it was Jamesy, threw a spud at him.

They both got up to fight, but the mother rapped the window at them, and they stooped again to the work, mumbling and muttering. From the head of the field came hearty laughter and immediately the two boys jumped to their feet. The father crooked up a protecting arm as the clods spattered around him. A stray bit of clay struck the window, bringing the mother into the garden. 'For goodness' sake, quit the capering! The neighbours'll think you're daft. Come in for yer tea the lot of ye. You've done plenty for wan day.'

They all sat in to the table, Rover begging from the floor, and jumping into the air for the bite of bread that Colm would throw to him. The door was open to the cool air and the lovely evening; through it the shadow of the house could be seen creeping up the byre wall opposite. Below on the shore gulls screeched in a mad flock, their wings catching gold from the evening; and up in the high field the sun shone upon the hay-ricks and stretched long shadows at their feet.

Paddy John Beg came in with a fishing-net over his shoulder and flung it on the floor. There were snail-lines on the flat corks and blackened seaweed clinging to one of the lead sinkers.

'The mice have it ate on me,' he said, pushing his hat back. 'I've been fixin' at it all the day. It was the divil's own job, but it'll do all right for the evenin'.'

He took a sup of tea in his hand, and when the sun had set, the two men went down to the shore, and Colm and Jamesy went off to the rock-heads to look for a stray sheep. Later they found her below the cliffs, and it was Rover that sent her racing madly up the path she had descended. When they reached the top of the cliff they scanned the sea for their father's boat and at last they saw her far out like a floating log.

That night as the mother lay in bed she thought how tired Daniel would be hauling nets after such a hard day's work in the garden. She heard the noise of rain against the window and she groped for her beads under the pillow and prayed that it would go over. But as she prayed she heard it falling heavily; it would be splashing now relentlessly on the shelterless boat, and high up on the lean hills sadly drenching the sheep and the growing lambs.

She got up and put coal and sods on the fire, and going to the door saw the bright beam of the lighthouse sweep through the drizzling night.

It was no use going to bed; she wouldn't sleep. She lifted the brush and began to sweep the floor. Rover lay stretched on an empty sack under the table and she brushed carefully round him. She tore the August leaf from the calendar on the wall and threw it into the fire. September, clean and glossy, stared at her, but she saw nothing only the 5th – the day Colm would be leaving. The old calendar leaf shrivelled in the flames and she gazed at it ruefully as if it were something personal that was burning.

Alec and Theresa gone; and now Colm would join them. But God was good; they were sensible children all of them; that was a blessing.

Letters stuck out from a cracked jug on the dresser and she took out some of Theresa's and some of Alec's. She knew the letters off by heart, but she read them again, glad to read that Alec's job was steady, and that Theresa had a good kind mistress; a pound a month wasn't much for a girl like Theresa, but sure she had her keep and that was a big thing.

She started when Rover gave a muffled growl; then he got up and went to the closed door, sniffed and wagged his tail. Soon Daniel came in, the brass eye-holes in his boots glistened, and fish-scales shone on his wet clothes.

'I came up for the cart, Mary. We've got a grand haul of herrin'.'

'Let them be till the mornin', sure yer foundered.'

'We're goin' early to Ballycastle with half of them and we

can salt the rest. I'll take over a bag of new spuds too; there may be a good price for them.'

'Wait for a drop of tea itself.'

'Paddy's waitin' for me,' he replied. 'I won't be long.'

She went out to help him tackle the horse and soon he was rattling down to the coast. She banked the fire and filled the kettle, and then stood at the door watching the lighthouse beam shrink in the whitening day. Morning wasn't far off; a red and violet sky glowed over the Scottish hill; a gull stirred and called; and a blue milky light chilled the island.

She unhooked the blind from the window, and the dog got up, yawned, and stretched himself.

When the men came back with the cart she had bowls of hot tea for them on the table. As they gulped the tea Mary told Daniel what to get her in Ballycastle: meat, wool, and four pounds of tea because they charged two prices for it on the island; and to buy himself a new pair of trousers for he was a disgrace at Mass on a Sunday.

When they were going off, a weak sun came out and spangled a wet-silver light upon the sea.

'Don't forget the meat,' she called after him; she'd have a nice dinner for them all on Sunday.

Gulls began to find their voices and cows lowed. It was going to be a grand day, thank God, and there was a nice air of wind to feed the sails.

Outside the door she gutted some herring while the uprising sun glistened over the soaked land and steam arose from the damp hay-ricks. It was a glittering morning. She shaded her eyes until the boat round Rue Point and was lost to view. She turned to the kitchen and filled a pan with herring, the sweet smell sending Colm and Jamesy leaping out of bed.

All the morning Colm and Jamesy gutted the herring, and later they went off to a shallow mountain lake to sail boats.

The boats were of different shapes and sizes: flat-pointed

sticks with goose feathers for sails; rusty tins bent into canoes; and a piece of a pig trough tacked with beams and made into a toy row boat. The ships skimmed across the lake, colliding with their cargoes of timber, coal, and flour. Sometimes one of the canoes, when the moping breeze burst upon it in sudden fury, would tip its cargo overboard and sink in glorious excitement.

In the early evening when the wind lost its warmth and the lake reddened under the sky, Colm sat exhausted on the bank. Rover dragged out stones from the water with his snout and placed them at Colm's feet. He barked loudly and wagged his tail, but Colm paid no heed to him. Beside him lay the wet boats with their feathers scrawly and thinned by the water. The wind raked the glowing surface of the lake and the waves rippled and broke in bubbles on the shore.

Jamesy was at the far end waiting for his last boat to come to port. Her rag of a sail had broken from the nail in the stern and now fluttered from the mast. He threw stones to hurry it along and when the dog jumped in after them he shouted wildly. Colm smiled at his eagerness, and idly he lifted one of the flat boats, took out the feather from the mast-hole and threw it on the ground. He sighed, for suddenly the thought of going away surged over him.

Jamesy retrieved the disabled boat and ran to the top of a hill from where he watched the sea. Then he turned to Colm in excitement. 'Colm! The boat! Here's the boat!'

He stretched out his hand and pointed. They looked away south and saw the brown-sailed boat as tiny as a floating leaf; it would be a while yet before she'd be in. They ran down to the house.

The mother hurried on with the meal and Clare was put to bed. Jamesy or Colm would run to the door and come in again with news of the boat's approach.

She put on her shawl and went down to the shore. Night clouds crowded on the horizon when the boat landed. The men were silent and she smelt the drink as the two of them sprawkled on to the rocks.

Colm and Jamesy carried the parcels between them. They tore little holes in the brown paper and peeped in. Colm carried a new pair of boots; they'd be for himself.

'You get everything and I get nothin',' whimpered Jamesy. Among the parcels that he carried he discovered sweets in a bag and a tin whistle. He was playing the whistle when the men stepped into the kitchen.

Mary rummaged through the parcels and clicked her teeth. 'Where's the meat, Dan?'

Daniel stood in the middle of the floor, his scummed eyes catching the lamplight, and his moustache wet with spittle. There was an expression of helplessness on his face and legs. He had left the meat behind him on the Ballycastle quay.

'A nice place to leave it,' she said, standing beside him and taking off his collar. 'Ye spent too much of yer time and too much of yer money in McAuley's pub I'm thinkin'.'

Jamesy began to finger the tin whistle and its watery notes bubbled into the air.

'Man, you'll fairly gather the seals with that,' said Paddy John Beg. 'They'll come slitherin' on to the rocks as soon as you whistle them.'

Jamesy sat beside him and pestered the tired man with questions about the seals and what tunes to play. He wanted to go down to the shore there and then, but Colm wouldn't go with him.

Daniel was listless at the meal, one arm drooped over the back of his chair.

'The good dinner goin' to loss,' said Mary, giving him a shake. 'Take the tea itself, Dan; it'll warm you up.'

But Daniel was half asleep. His breath wheezed in his nose and his head fell forward on his chest.

'Has he much in him?' she asked Paddy.

'Aw, now, Mary, not very much. A few bottles – that's all.'

She brought Dan up to the room and saw him into bed and when she came back Paddy John Beg was in lively form. He was lighting his pipe, pressing the match-box down on the bowl, and puffing out great clouds of smoke. Jamesy was still asking about the seals, but his mother had taken the whistle and put it away on the dresser.

Jamesy left Paddy over a bit of the road and held on to his arm.

'And will the seals come as soon as I whistle?'

'They'll come, man, like hens to a handful of corn.'

Paddy groped amongst the coins in his pocket, fingering their edges until he found a penny.

'Buy sweets for yourself with that,' and he squeezed it into Jamesy's hand.

That night Colm awakened with a start and saw chinks of light in the partition and heard stifled groans from his father. He raised his head from the pillow and listened intently; it was very still. His mother moved about in the kitchen and water splashed in a basin. He sat up in the bed. His mother was talking in soft tones. 'Is that any aisier, Dan?'

Colm came into the room in his shirt. 'Is he bad, mother?' he asked and his teeth chattered.

'No, no; he's got a chill and he'll be all right. G'on back to your bed, son, or you'll get your death of cold.'

The mother placed a brick on the fire and covered it with ashes and when it was well-heated she wrapped it in a flannel and put it at Daniel's feet; later he dozed off to sleep.

FIVE

Throughout the next few days Daniel was still in bed, cooped up in the little room. The days were fiercely hot and the blue skies were grained with twirls of cloud. Heat shimmered over the bean fields and wriggled like flame-shadow above the rocks. Cows crushed into the thin shade of the hedges and swished the clegs madly with their tails. Up on the hills the lakes shrunk and left a web of dry mud-cracks on the edges. Grasshoppers sizzled all day long in the heather. Hens scratched holes at the side of the byre; and Rover panted in the shadow of the heeled-up cart.

The sea lay in a hot calm. On the shore sea-rods whitened and crusted with salt; flies bunched around decaying heads of dog-fish; and rotten seaweed stagnated in the warm air. Fresh tar on the boats bubbled and blistered; and captured flies rotted in the spiders' webs.

But in the MacNeill cottage a chill had crept in with Daniel's sickness. Voices became whispers and the boys tiptoed about in their bare feet. On the top of the dresser lay the tin whistle.

In the cool of the evenings the swallows skimmed over the fields and clustered noisily about the byre eaves. And when night came the woodwork creaked in the sick man's room, and in the stillness he could hear now and again the heart pulse of a ship's engine coming through the quiet air.

Sweat itched his forehead and warm air heaved against the four-paned window. The heat of the room was as thick as bed-clothes; and time and again Mary would look with scorn at the sealed window when she'd hear his crackling breath. All day she sat beside his bed watching the quick rise and fall of the clothes, bathing his brow and whisking the flies away that lit on his forehead; and once when a blue bottle buzzed against the window she slipped across the room and crushed it in the towel.

Next day Father Byrne got her to send to Ballycastle for the doctor. The doctor arrived in a motor-boat and hurried to the house. Daniel had pneumonia. He was far through and too weak to be moved to hospital.

'Why wasn't I sent for earlier?' the doctor asked.

'I thought it was only a bad cold,' Mary answered him brokenly.

'He must have air anyway,' and taking his stick he smashed two panes in the window.

A week passed. Aunt Maggie came up from the lower end of the island to help, but Daniel took a turn for the worse. They wired to Alec and Theresa; and Colm went over with the island men to meet them.

It was a dull clumsy day with rainy clouds thatching the island and a moist wind blowing from the southwest. They sat waiting at Ballycastle quay; it was better to wait there than go trooping round the town and maybe miss them.

When Alec and Theresa arrived on the quay they were flushed from hurrying. The boat was ready. Paddy John

Beg gripped Alec's hand and looked away from him. Alec knew by the quiet greeting and the silence of the men that his father was bad. He found himself asking how he was.

'Don't worry, Alec,' Paddy was saying. 'He'll pull through with the help of God. Daniel's a wiry one.'

They pushed out at once. Alec sat beside Colm in the stern and asked him the age-old questions: Was he lying long? Was the priest with him? Did they get the doctor? When he heard that his father was anointed he knew that it was touch and go.

Theresa sat in the bow with the collar of her black raincoat turned up, and her brown hat dusted with rain. Her face was grieved; she held her head down, looking at a handkerchief stretched between her hands. When Colm looked up at her she smiled wanly. Now and again as she'd turn her head towards the island she'd choke back a cry and crush the handkerchief with her hands.

Alec fidgeted. He lit a cigarette, took a few pulls at it, and then threw it into the sea. Colm saw it for a moment rise on the back of a wave and vanish on the crest; in his mind he saw the paper burst and the tobacco strands spill out upon the sea.

The rain ceased and Alec looked anxiously at the peak of the sail flapping loosely in the wind. He threw off his coat and stuck an oar over the side. He was stockily built and immense in the shoulders. His hair was fair and thin, his face brick red, and his eyes intensely blue. As he pulled at the oar he stretched his legs against the beam in front and the veins hardened on his hands. He pulled for a long time and then some of the men gave him a spell.

It was late in the evening when they coaxed the boat along the blackening shore. The mists had lifted and the sea lay calm. There was no sound of life from the island except the clopping of the waves and the bleating of sheep from the cliff-tops. But down at the port a few people had gathered to meet the boat.

'He's far through, Alec; he's far through,' said someone as Alec jumped ashore. 'The priest is in with him.'

They began to run. People were kneeling outside the door and they edged to one side, their eyes softened with sorrow as Alec and Theresa passed them.

The room was crowded; it was hot with kneeling people. The mother stood at the side of the bed holding the lighted candle in Daniel's hand. Alec and Theresa and Colm knelt near her.

Daniel's eyes were open, but they didn't move; the sight was leaving them. Colm's lips quivered; his prayers were breath rather than sound; his heart thumped loudly from the running and he became clammy with sweat.

A moth came in through the splintered window and circled round the candle; the flame trembled as the people answered the prayers. Drops of melted wax trickled down the sides of the candle and hardened in a dull cord.

Mary bent and closed Daniel's eyes, and then a long whine from her broke over the kneeling people. Alec caught her in his arms.

'Let her empty herself,' said an old woman. 'It'll ease her heart, the craythure.'

Colm slipped past the people at the door and went to his den at the back of the hill. The rain-wet grass was cold under his bare feet, and through his tears he saw the stars needled with gold. It was dark, but he wasn't afraid of it now. He shivered and nervous tremors convulsed his body.

All the little nameless things that had brought his own life in contact with his father's crowded in his mind: occasions when he had disobeyed him; not going to the shop for tobacco; hiding when he wanted him to dig scraws on the hill; and a day he raced off to hunt rabbits when his father, plastering the byre-gable, wanted him to fetch sand from the shore. He clenched his fist to keep back the tears, but they burst upon him with great violence, and he sat on the cold ground, heedless of his surroundings, his whole being gnawed with grief.

Down at the cottage the people were leaving in ones and twos, going out into the night-air along the paths and roads that led from the house, the old people slow on the road, their minds clutched with the thought of death, their hands groping secretly for their beads; but as the young receded from the gloomy house their voices gradually grew louder, thinking of the wake and the yarns that would be told and the sup of free drink on the rounds.

SIX

The corn and barley ripened early; the beans and hay were safely stored; and then blighting mists and black frosts swirled over the land. Daniel's grave had lost its freshness and nothing remained on the mound except a circular rusted wire that once held a wreath of flowers.

Winter came. Winds and rain burst upon the island and the cattle were driven into the shelter of the byres. Waves pounded the shoulders of rock and littered the shore with sea-rods and gleaming wrack.

At night Paddy John Beg came over to the MacNeill cottage for a ceilidh. Theresa had gone back to her job in Belfast, but Alec remained at the fishing and the farm. There were dances and cards in the school-house, but Daniel was not long enough in his grave for the MacNeills to be seen sporting themselves.

Colm was still at home. Alec had scoffed at the idea of sending him to college and time and again Father Byrne pleaded with him saying he'd not have to spend a penny on his education.

'He's needed here, Father,' Alec had said. 'I want to get away myself and the farm will fall to him.'

'You're doing the child a gross injustice,' Father Byrne had answered, 'and some day you'll rue it.'

In the dark wintry mornings Alec and Colm and Jamesy were up early, and the frozen dawn would see them along the wet stones of the shore gathering into heaps the tangled sea-rods and searching in the rocky gullets for wreckage. They worked hard; by the early summer they'd have plenty of kelp for the kilns. Sometimes Alec would shelter in a cave for a smoke and rail against the island.

'We'd all be better in the town,' he'd say. 'Sure there's nothin' here for anyone, workin' like slaves at the kelp and gettin' damn all for it in the end. And look at the land, the spongy look of it would give you cramps in your belly.'

And then he'd talk to them about Ireland and how the people long ago were robbed of their lands; or standing on a hill he'd turn towards the mainland and tell how the good land was in the hands of the planters and the old Irish scattered like sheep among the mountains and the rocks.

When a newspaper was sent to him he'd read about the Home Rulers, Sinn Féiners, and election fights in Belfast and other parts of the country. 'Good God, to think of it,' he said. 'Here we are on a farl of rock doing nothing for our country except whining and whinging. There's nothing to fight here. We must be a gutless clutch of orderly people when we haven't even a peeler to look after us. Times I wonder whether we're Irish at all sitting here between Ireland and Scotland; nobody's darling and nobody wantin' us.' And then he burst out laughing and went on with the work again.

When Alec talked like this, Colm and Jamesy would look at him in a puzzled way, their minds trying to piece together the scattered stories of Ireland's history they had learnt at school. But they never questioned their right to a better land; they loved the fishing and the excitement of finding a box or a log washed up on the shore.

And then one night in early January a fog covered the island and the sea. All through the night Alec heard the rockets of the lighthouse shattering and echoing through the thick fog, and every minute boats' sirens mooing like distressed cattle. He could tell by the volume of sound how close they were to the shore. Through the fogged window he saw the lighthouse pale as a frosted moon; its beam could travel no distance in that thickness.

He couldn't sleep with the noise of the rockets and the hooting of the boats; he groped for his pipe and matches. Barely had he lit the pipe than a tearing, crashing sound shook the house; and then the continuous, uninterrupted screech from a boat's whistle sent him hurrying out of bed.

His mother got up at the noise. She hammered the partition.

'I think there's a boat ashore, Alec.'

'I hear her,' he shouted. 'I'll go over for Paddy.'

'What time of the night is it at all?' she asked.

He struck a match and looked at the face of his watch. 'It's half-six, it won't be long till dawn and the fog may lift then.'

When he opened the door wrinkles of fog eddied in the kitchen, and the hooting of the siren came so clear that the boat seemed to be below the very house. Dogs barked; the whole island must be astir. He lit a candle in the byre and lifted an old hurricane lamp from a peg in the wall; it was looped with cobwebs and dusted with flakes of limewash. He wiped it with a piece of a sack and filled it with oil.

Voices of youths were loud as they passed by on the road. They were all talking at once and asking where was she ashore.

Paddy John Beg arrived. 'We better go down to the

rocket station, the men will be gathering there.'

Alec and Paddy set off together through the thick, black fog. The hurricane lamp threw a blurred circle of light on the road and the frosted breath of the fog glowed dustily around it. The fog wetted their hair and clung to their faces like cobwebs.

When they came near the village they heard the crunch of the small life-saving cart on the stones and men shouting orders as they pulled it. Lamps were dotted here and there like the port-holes on a ship at night. Men walked in front, marking the way. Everyone was talking; and over all came the loud, low note of the ship's horn.

'She has plenty of steam up,' said Paddy to Alec. 'She must be a big one.'

Youths came running to say she was ashore at Alley. Johnny McQuilkin, in charge of the life-saving apparatus, kept shouting at the men to hurry.

When they reached the low cliffs at Alley the fog had thinned. The whole island seemed to be gathered about the cliff and above the chatter came the stunning hoot from the ship's horn.

Johnny McQuilkin put a megaphone to his mouth and hailed. His voice was dulled by the fog and the horn. He shouted again; there was no reply. Then he told them to give her a rocket.

A rocket whizzed into the blue fog. The fine rope was hauled in again; it had missed. Taking another a rocket was fired again. Six times it whizzed into the air, but without result.

And then the last puff of steam silenced the whistle and a great hollowness spread over the island, but in the ears of the men its ghostly sound still lingered. Other ships were close to the shore, blowing frantically.

Slowly like mist from a polished mirror the fog thinned, showing a black ship tilted on the submerged rocks below the low cliff. The life-line was fired right across her but no one on the ship came to it. Johnny McQuilkin shouted again through the megaphone, and then he noticed large toothed gaps on her deck where her life-boats had rested.

'The crew must have put to sea,' he said.

The men stood about awkwardly on the cliff-top looking at the boat with her black and white-rimmed funnel and the water frothing around her stern; she was caught between two pincers of rock. As they watched, the fog tore itself into strands and far out from the shore could be seen two steamers and the small life-boats from the grounded ship making for them.

'It bates all how she managed in there,' Paddy John Beg was saying to Alec, 'and the whole wide sea to travel on.'

'In two weeks she'll be a total wreck,' said Alec.

Paddy winked at him and smiled. 'In two hours she'll be stripped as clean as a whistle, I'm thinkin'.'

The two steamers gathered up the lifeboats and sailed towards the Scottish coast. And then as if obeying some communal instinct the men moved off, leaving the cliff to the women and children.

Alec sent Colm and Jamesy up to the house for a hatchet, a screwdriver, and all the ropes that they could find. And while they were racing up to the house they saw other boys scampering as hard as they could to their homes.

In half an hour the island boats were moving out in ones and twos to the ship, gathering round it like wasps to a nest.

'May as well have what's on her than let the sea swallow it,' they were saying.

'Take what the sea sends and be thankful,' Paddy said to Alec.

'She's heavily insured,' Alec answered. 'And it's the good God that sent her to us.'

Alec was the first to clamber on board and he dangled a rope over the side and staked his claim. Colm and Jamesy held the row-boat out from the ship's side. Men were climbing on to her from all sides and soon there was nothing but hammering and tramping. Alec screwed off two heavy brass clocks and Paddy appeared with a table on his head and threw it into the sea where it floated with its legs up.

'That's ours, Colm, son,' he shouted. 'Tie a rope to it, ye needn't bring it aboard.'

Alec came with parcels and boxes, tied them with ropes, and lowered them into the row-boat, and when she was laden Paddy helped the boys to row her to the port. The table towed badly and Paddy cut it adrift and said that it would wash ashore.

The mother and Uncle Robert were waiting to inspect the first cargo and as soon as the bundles were placed on the stones the mother put a hand to her mouth and exclaimed, 'Merciful God in Heaven, such a fortune!' Uncle Robert sat smoothing his stick and watched with feigned indifference the boxes being lifted out of the boat. Then he got up and prodded the parcels with his stick and got down on his knees to read the print on the boxes.

'Thread,' he would say scornfully. 'Soap. Flannel.' And then he'd yell, 'Is there no whiskey aboard her at all? I know by the look of her snout that she's a Scotch boat. Man, dear, if I were supple again it's warmth I'd bring ashore.'

Colm and Jamesy were too excited to listen to him. They were eager to get back again, and they'd turn their heads towards the steamer and shout the names of the boats that had the biggest loads.

Soon they were on their way again. The sea was littered with paper and empty boxes. They waved and called gleefully to boys in other boats. One boy held up a melodeon and started to play; and when Jamesy reached the vessel he kept shouting to Alec to get him a melodeon. But

Alec paid no heed to him. He had bags and boxes bulging over the lip of the steamer. Two men began to fight, but no one went near them.

All day long the islanders worked at the ship. Doors and planks smacked into the sea, and some men put marks of tar on them so that they could claim them when they'd be washed ashore. Buckets of coal were lowered last, and by nightfall the ship was as draughty as an old disused cow shed.

The next day they rummaged thorough their wares. Alec found he had enough tobacco to do him a life-time; the mother had as much thread as would make a net for the world; Colm and Jamesy had a telescope between them to look at boats by day and stars by night; and Clare amused herself with a wash-hand basin that was propped on two stones outside the door. She loved to fill it with water, lift out the rubber stopper, and catch the outflow in a tin canister.

The following Sunday at Mass there wasn't a barefooted child on the whole island. Men and women had new coats of all shapes and sizes. Rosie Doherty had a fox fur draping her shoulders, and when Paddy John Beg saw her he nearly choked with laughing and told Alec that it wouldn't be an islander she'd be wanting now with that animal on her neck.

When Father Byrne turned to read the notices he felt that it was a foreign congregation he was addressing, and time and again almost burst out laughing. When he started to talk about the gallant effort that they had made to save the crew they didn't know whether he was humorous or satirical. Later Colm told at home how the priest had laughed his sides off after the Mass that morning.

Not long after the wreckage of the ship Father Byrne came to Alec again and pleaded with him to send Colm to the college. Alec softened, and on a cold day in the middle of January Colm left the island for Belfast.

BOOK TWO

THE CITY

'Frost will not touch the hedge of fuchsias,
The land will remain as it was,
But no abiding content can grow out of these minds
Fuddled with blood, always caught by blinds . . .'

LOUIS MacNEICE
'Valediction'

ONE

The college bell rang through the wet-cold air and boys, red from playing football or handball, ran from the fields. Sweat broke out on them and they rubbed their faces with handkerchiefs and clustered round the fountain for a drink, not taking time to fill the chained tumbler, but clugging their mouths to the brass jet.

The damp corridor was filled with their chatter as they hurried along. The red and blue tiles were mud-streaked by their feet, and on the moist glossy walls some boys had drawn faces with their fingers. Hot breaths rose in a mist above them and voices quietened as they neared the Study Hall.

Outside in the grey evening lay two playing fields, black with mud, the goal-posts white and dirtied by smacks from the ball. On one side was the dark jail wall, and on the opposite side the top windows of terrace houses overlooked the grounds. The fields were desolate, and already the gulls were swarming and calling as they lit on the ground.

Inside, the Study Hall glowed with dry warmth from the hot pipes. All the boys stood at their yellow desks waiting for the priest to enter. Some were combing their wet-streaked hair and others exchanging twopenny detective stories. Father McGorey came in. The fellows were glad: he was an easy man that read his breviary all the time or maybe perused a book that he'd find on a boy's desk. He ascended the rostrum. They blessed themselves. The priest began:

Direct, we beseech Thee, O Lord, all our actions and carry them on by Thy gracious assistance, that every prayer, word and work of ours may begin through Thee, and by Thee be happily ended through Christ Our Lord . . . Amen!

There was a loud shuffling of feet, a creaking of desks, and a turning of pages. Then silence.

At a point where four parallel rows of hot pipes entered the wall Colm sat, and yesterday, feeling a draught rubbing round his legs he had stuffed an old cap into the spaces, but someone had removed it. And now as he felt the chilly breeze blow in he tore pages from a scribbler and shoved them into the gap. Satisfied, he lifted the lid of his desk, rested it on his head, allowing his two hands freedom to rummage. He had been only three weeks in the College and already was thinking of Easter. On the underside of the lid a small calendar was fastened with drawing pins, and each date as it passed was totally obliterated by a square of ink. He began to count the days till Easter: there were forty-three, and to make it an even forty he scored out three in advance.

It seemed a long time since the wintry day he left the island: the row at Ballycastle station because his mother couldn't get him a half-ticket: seeing the snow on Knocklayde from the train, frozen fields with ragged bushes and no cattle, black streams with snow on the stones that stuck up through them; villages hushed and cartwheel marks on the roads; thatched houses stiff in the ground and hayricks huddled in the haggards and dusted with snow; and then as the train raced along by the edge of a thin sea into Belfast, seeing at one side trams with tin advertisements, and boys sliding on a pond whose top was littered with stones.

And then the drive up from the station in the side-car with his mother. How frightened he had been of the motor cars, and the frantic rattling of the car wheels on the street. He had held on grimly, listening to the driver clicking his tongue at the horse, his great bulk perched high on the dicky seat, and the hair on his neck fringing his coat collar. As they turned off the tram lines into the avenue that led to the wine-bricked College the wheels had quietened, and within him he had felt an emptiness that crushed all life from him. Thinking of it now he felt again the same gripping loneliness and he gave a long, loud sigh. The boy in front turned round and Colm smiled back at him with his lips closed.

He put his hand in his pocket for a pencil and his fingers touched a green marble pebble which Jamesy had given him the day he left the island. He took it out and looked at it in the palm of his hand. It was polished from rubbing against the things in his pocket; he turned it over admiring its tiny vein of white and its freckles of brown; and as he looked at it a shore took shape in his mind: grey stones in a curve, and down by the edge of the tide the pebbles rattling as the waves came slashing in, farther back dry sticks eaten by sea lice, a frayed piece of rope, whitened limpet shells that crackled under the feet, and a bicycle tyre with rusted rims ... A creak of boots made his fist close on the pebble while his free hand opened the pages of a book. Father McGorey passed by reading his breviary.

Colm wanted to be alone. The smell of burnt dust on the hot pipes gave him a headache, and when the priest turned again and came towards him, Colm raised his hand.

'Sure, you're only in,' said the priest quietly.

'But, Father, I have a headache,' replied Colm, trying to look as meek as he could.

'Go for a little walk round the track, and don't be long.'

Once outside on the hard cinder track the evening air braced him a little. A greyness covered the sky and darkness was coming. Colm left the track and took the wet-black path that wriggled under the bare trees, now dripping with rain.

He was glad it was raining. He sat on the mouldy-green seat with a granite wall behind him glossy with rain. The seat was damp and hacked with boys' names. He felt the slime oozing through to him, but he didn't move, hoping that he would get sick and maybe be sent home early. Beads of fungi like lentils grew on the legs of the seat and he idly knocked them off with his toe, his mind weaving life-patterns with the names carved out on the seat – J.H. 1911: M. Scally: M.B.

Above his head the scraggy branches of a tree clutched at the wind and now and again drops fell to the sunken leaves at his feet: spit, spat, spit, spat. Their rhythmic sound stirred a memory of the death candle in his father's grip, the star-like splash of grease as it fell warm and then cooled on his mother's hand – warm tears from a candle, cold tears from the sky: spit, spat, spit, spat. He found himself swallowing a lump in his throat and he breathed: God have mercy on my father's soul. He blinked his eyes and the thought faded from his mind.

A gull called and skimmed shadow-like across the field. His eyes followed it closely, thinking of the ripples of air streaming from its breast and sliding round its tail. He wondered where they went at night, whether they stayed in the college grounds or flew off to the sea. Just then they all arose slowly, glided over the jail wall and he saw them no more.

It was suddenly dusk. Colm got up. As he walked round

the track he noticed a flutter of a handkerchief from a corner window of the jail. A prisoner was playfully waving to him. The handkerchief shook, stopped, and tossed again. Colm raised his arm, and now the handkerchief shook frantically. He stood and signalled for a while and then turned towards the College, sometimes looking back to wave. When he entered the corridor the handkerchief was still fluttering like a captured gull against the grey stone of the jail.

The corridor was dark, but the lights were lit in the study hall, and there was the smell of a new gas mantle above his desk. The fabric of an old mantle lay on the lid and he blew it away with his breath before sitting down.

He was cold and felt refreshed. Father McGorey saw the happy look on his face and he walked between the desks, wagging his hands behind his back and feeling pleased at having sent the island lad for a little walk.

Colm opened his book and read the first sum . . .

A man starts from A and rows upstream: $1\frac{1}{2}$ miles above A he passes a bottle floating down; after another 18 mins he turns back and arrives at A at the same moment as the bottle. If his speed through the water and the speed of the stream are both uniform, find the speed of the stream in miles per hour.

He neatly wrote down: *Let x = speed of stream* in mls/hr.

But he could get no further; he could see no sense in it; and he allowed his mind to wander from the sums out to the fluttering handkerchief and wonder who the prisoner was, what was he in jail for, and where did he come from. No one knew about the prisoner but himself; he rejoiced in the secret and decided to ask out tomorrow to signal again to the prisoner. With his pen he began to draw boats and lighthouses.

Father McGorey passed close beside him, his soutane making a little stir of air. Colm looked up at the back of the priest, at the soutane shiny round the shoulder-blades and the dandruff on the neck. Then his eyes rested on the large crucifix that stood in a niche at the top of the study hall. The pale tortured body of Our Saviour was patterned with the shadow of a gas-bracket. To the left was a large clock. Study was nearly over. Colm had nothing done; it was the same every day; he never seemed to get anything done. In the morning he always got up when the bell rang, but after he had washed and brushed his boots, he found that he was always the last to leave the dormitory.

He turned again to his sums about the 'streams', but he could get no answers. He could tell the master in the morning that he tried them. A bell rang. Study was over for an hour.

Fellows rushed out to the daffs for a quick smoke and then hurried back to the refectory for a cup of cocoa and hunks of bread. The cocoa was sweetish and it made Colm both warm and sick. He tried to take it in gulps so that he wouldn't taste its sweetness, but it caught in his throat and he burst into a fit of uncontrollable coughing. A boy beside him thumped him on the back and everyone burst out laughing. Colm felt ashamed of himself and when he felt the coughs coming again he gripped the chair tightly and swallowed the hiccups till a vein on his forehead stood out like a cord.

Back in the study hall again an odd cough would come from him as he learned his French and Latin declensions. These done he turned again to his sums, prayed to St Anthony to help him, but nothing happened; he could get no further than . . . *Let x = time to swim upstream.*

Men swimming and men rowing were still in his mind as he climbed the steep, stone steps to the chapel for night-prayers. Boys nodded to him, but as yet he had made no friends.

The diminutive plaster figures of saints panelled at the base of the altar distracted him. Their beards were all holed like a cheap sponge and when he blinked his eyes in a certain way he imagined he saw the little figures coming to life and jigging to and fro. Tonight he closed his eyes altogether, bent his head, and tried to feel the prayers as they chorused them after the monitor . . .

Behold, O good and most sweet Jesus, I cast myself upon my knees in thy sight, and with the most fervent desire of my soul I pray and beseech thee that Thou wouldst imprint on my heart lively sentiments of faith, hope, and charity, with true repentance for my sins and a firm desire of amendment; whilst with deep affection and grief of soul I ponder within myself and mentally contemplate thy five most precious wounds, having before my eyes that which David spake concerning thee, O good Jesus, they have dug my hands and my feet, they have numbered all my bones.

As Colm recited the prayer he saw a contorted Christ upon the Cross on a mountain, the purple blood dripping over the Sacred Face, spurting from His side, and trickling down the base of the Cross into the stony socket. He sighed when the prayer was over.

In silence they said their own private prayers; and then noisily down the steps again, tramping along the bleakly lit corridor with its cold breeze blowing through it, into the vestibule, setting their cheap watches by the grandfather clock, and up the stairs that led to the dark dormitories, dark because of the double rows of yellow cubicles like horse-boxes. Boys clambered round the row of jets washing their teeth. They shuffled about on their feet to keep themselves warm. Colm had no toothbrush, and after borrowing three matches he hurried into bed.

He lay awake listening to the noises dying down: a stud dropping on the wooden floor; a bed creaking as someone turned in it; and someone making a gusty sound as he stretched his feet into the cold part of the bed. Away high up near the roof he heard the slatted ventilator tearing two notes from the rising wind, and opposite the bed saw the stars frosting the bare window.

When all was still he got up quietly, went to the window, and looked towards the jail. The moon was shining on its grey walls, the windows were black, but no sign of a light in the prisoner's end. The two playing fields were desolate, with the gulls gone and the goal-posts coldly white. On a puddle of water on the path the moon shone and when the breeze scuffled the surface the light rippled and broke in many fragments. Colm in his long nightshirt watched the wind coming and going across the puddle, and now and again raised anxious eyes towards the jail. But no sign of the prisoner came to him.

He went from the window and got his matches. He lit one and held it in the red bowl of his hands and moved it up and down. Three times he lit the matches and signalled, but there was no response, and then as he turned away he found himself beside Father McGorey, an electric torch in his hand and a cane by his side.

'What are you doing here?' he said in a loud whisper. 'Trying to set the building on fire when everyone's asleep?'

Colm crushed the spent matches in his hand. The smell of sulphur seemed to be all round the dormitory. His teeth chattered.

'Report to me in the morning, and get into bed before you get your death.'

Colm got back into bed again. Father McGorey patted him on the head with his cigarette-smelling fingers.

'Good night, now,' he said and slipped away.

The priest's carpet slippers padded down the dormitory; a loose board sagged under his weight; and the wind whistled as a door opened and shut. The smell of the priest's fingers still lingered about the pillow and into Colm's mind there came a picture of Alec throwing the cigarette into the waves, the paper bursting, and the yellow threads spilling out upon the sea . . .

TWO

The days dragged, brightened now and then by a letter
from home, telling how Rover had missed him, how
Clare was growing a big girl, that Jamesy intended putting
in the potatoes himself this year, and how Uncle Robert was
asking about him and hoped to see him back again at Easter.
Colm carried these letters in his pocket and at odd moments
when homesickness would surge over him he would sneak
under the trees and read them over and over again. His
mother had seldom mentioned Alec, and he wondered if he
still begrudged the island its existence. He often talked to his
companions about his home and the boats and fishing, so
that by talking he could bring its life close to him.

His first free day when the boarders were allowed out he
made his way to the docks to see the ships. Their huge red
funnels, white paint-work and varnished masts filled him
with delight. At the other side of the harbour were the coal-
boats, the crane buckets descending into their bowels and

disgorging shining pyramids of coal on the quay. Over the Queen's Bridge lines of coal-carts rattled; trams mumbled; and once a donkey passed drawing a cart of steaming coal-brick. Colm stood on the bridge counting the big cross-channel boats, looking at the Lagan water swirling round the quoins of the bridge, holding captive in one corner orange peel, straw, and empty cigarette packets. From the opposite side of the bridge he saw coming down the river barges laden with turf-mould and going to dock under a black shed which had on the roof big white letters – PEAT, MOSS, LITTER. He wished with all his heart that Jamesy was with him.

On his way back to the College he wandered about the city learning the names of the streets: Oxford Street, Victoria Street, Cromac Street, Durham Street, Townshend Street, Carlisle Circus, and he thought of the island names – Lagavristeevore, Killaney, Crocnacreeva, Carnasheeran, Crocaharna – words full of music, and he said them aloud to himself as he went along.

The following Thursday about four o'clock Theresa called for him to bring him to the pictures. The president allowed him to go and told him to get a hair-cut when he was out, otherwise they would have to put a ribbon and plaits in it. The tracks of the comb were in his wet hair when he joined his sister at the door and made off down the avenue. They walked slowly, and then Theresa caught Colm by the arm.

'Do you know who's at the gate? . . . Joe Heaney,' she said and turned her head away. 'He's going to bring the two of us to the pictures. Be nice to him, Colm. I'll tell you about him again.'

About twelve yards from the gate Joe Heaney stood, a grey cap on his head, a cigarette in his mouth, and his hands in the pockets of a navy-blue suit. He was clean-shaven and he wore a new white collar.

'This is Colm, Joe,' said Theresa as the three of them walked towards a tram-stop. He shook hands tightly with Colm, grunted something, and looked away. They stood at the tram-stop and an awkward silence came over them. Theresa could find no words to say; Joe peered up the road and nicked the cigarette on the heel of his boot; and Colm wished that he was back in the College. But once within the darkness of the picture house he forgot about Joe as he followed a South Seas film. It had all ended too quickly and when they came out to the lights of the city, his eyes felt heavy and sleepy, and Joe began talking about the picture. They went into an ice-cream shop, and afterwards Colm went off along to get a hair-cut.

Theresa called to see him again on her next evening off. They met in the cold little reception room that had always frilled green paper in the black-leaded grate. The room was dull in the dying daylight. Theresa had a paper bag of cheap buns for him. She talked all the time about Joe.

'He's crazy about me,' she said. 'And he likes you. He may get a good job in Birmingham in some motor works and give me the ring at Easter ... He thinks you're a nice wee fella, but very shy, and I told him how clever you were.'

'What'd you do that for?' Colm answered crossly. 'Now he'll go and tell everybody things that aren't true ... I'm a dunce. I can do nothing in this place, and if you want to know, I'm the worst in the class.'

'Sure I didn't know, Colm,' she said pleadingly. 'I just wanted to show Joe that we were decent people and had a brother at College ... Don't let on to him that Father Byrne's paying for you. I don't tell Joe everything.'

Colm sulked, and when she was ready to go she gave him sixpence. 'If I had more I'd give it to you. I'm only getting twenty-five shillings a month and my keep. But I'll knit you stockings after I get a pair for Joe finished.'

Colm watched her go away from him. He put the bag of

buns under his coat and went into the corridor to look for Chit McCloskey.

He had two companions now, one boarder, Chit McCloskey, and a day-boy, Jimmy Millar. It was always in the mornings at Religious Instruction that he met Millar. Millar had two false teeth and when he got the master's back turned he would wink at Colm, open his mouth and move the false teeth up and down with his tongue. Colm often laughed at him, and when the master lifted the cane Millar sat still, his mouth closed tightly, and his black eyes full of innocence.

Religious Instruction was easy. The master, usually a priest, talked for twenty minutes and never asked a question. The fellows loved this class, and with a book below the desk they secretly learned their Latin declensions.

Colm now disliked Latin. All the feeling that the old island priest had put into an image of Nature or a lovely thought had vanished in the search for the verb, the rules of syntax, the emphasis on the word and not the phrase. The lines in the Latin verse were dissected, the master saying, 'Mark that, boys, that's a likely passage for the Examination!'

And then, because he had come to the College when the first term was over, he had to attend a grind class held by Father Alby, a big fat man with a shiny head, hunched shoulders and a shabby soutane. He had to teach the class for forty minutes every day in all subjects. He always swept into the room a few minutes late, the door banging behind him. He pounded on the dais, put a pile of books down on the little table, and then stood cogitating with one hand on his hinch. He would lift one of the books, open and bang it shut so as to clear the dust of it, and then stare at the rigid faces upturned to him.

'Now we'll have some grammar, then geography, history, geometry, and if there's time, a little algebra ... Attention!'

Twenty boys stiff with attention tried to stiffen a little more. They watched every movement of him, and when a little breeze blew in from the diamond-paned windows the few strands of hair on Alby's head stood up and slowly fell back again. Colm often watched the hair rising and he had a queer notion that as soon as Alby lost those few hairs he would die.

The master smoothed the top of his hairs with the palm of his hand and shouted: 'Take out yer Shakespeares! You read, Millar!'

Millar read a few lines, was told to stop and to parse every word. Nobody could understand parsing, but Alby loved to pound it into them. Everything was parsed: strong verbs, weak verbs, gerunds, and moods.

Then the map of Ireland was rolled down the wall and the master with a long pointer in his hand stood at the side like a Roman centurion. He would look to the south of the map, turn round quickly, and ask a boy to point out Moville and Tory Island. The boy would come out and maybe peer around the south of Ireland in his search for Moville. 'Ah-ha,' Alby would say. 'And you thought Moville was in the County Cork, and there's it there in the extreme North.'

And then he would go into his daily chants: 'Here I am wasting my sweetness on desert air. You blocks, you gumps, you worse than senseless things!'

'How did you come by those yellow fingers ... Smoke! Smoke! Smoke! You are rotten with cigarettes ... What would your parents say if they knew? ... Avaunt and quit my sight, you scurvy fellows!'

'Ah-ha, with my biting cane I'll make you skip,' or looking towards a boy who was dreaming, 'He's scarce awake; let him alone awhile.'

Then before he would go out: 'One word more ... Did I give you an exercise for today? ... Methinks I hear Millar whinge and MacNeill groan.'

And then round the class looking at the exercises, the crack of his cane denoting his progress. 'Is this an exercise I see before me, the scrawly writing toward my hand? Come here, boy!'

Slowly he would pass round, listening incredulously to some boys who had no exercise done.

'Where's your exercise?'

'I have a sore finger and I couldn't hold the pen.'

'Please, boy, undo this bandage.'

'And had Tom a-cold. Poor Tom!'

When the forty minutes were up he went out. The fellows exhaled audibly and a buzz of talk slowly filled the room.

Then Father Daly came in for English. He was a small man with sleek black hair and a bony face. The boys talked freely while he took out his watch, rubbed the face of it with this thumb, and placed it on the table. For a minute he sat thinking, then with a slow movement he took out the strips of paper that marked his books, opened them, and turned them over.

'We'll have today,' he said in his quiet voice, 'a little story that I came across and then I'll read for you some poetry.'

It was the same every day, stories to read and interesting things to do. The fellows rubbed their hands with delight, sat up, and listened to Father Daly as he read about an old man selling pictures in Cork. And he read for them old Gaelic poems about winter and snow, spring and birds.

But the class listened to him inattentively when he talked about the use of words; 'You judge a poet by the words he uses. If he uses tired words, stale words, he's a bad poet,' and he took passages from Shakespeare to show how he had used words.

'If you write about your own lives, your own homes,' he continued, 'you'll probably write well, for it belongs to literature to express this life and to express it with feeling.'

He condemned Examinations: 'They're the curse of all

real feeling.' And because he did not give his pupils the official Examination essays – '*My favourite Character in History*', '*Dogs and Cats as Pets*', '*Influence of Climate on Character*', '*Honesty*' – his class always did badly.

Today, because it was March and a blue wind bumped the windows, he got them to write a poem on March and offered a shilling for the best.

Colm thought of the daffodils that printed ST KEVIN'S on the shelving bank of the playing field, and how from the other end of the field one could see the large yellow letters, each taller than a man. Then he began to write about the frosty winds shaking the slender stalks and the little creepers hiding in the throats of the flowers; evening comes; the flowers close for the night; the creepers are captured, to be released again by the sun in the morning.

Colm won the shilling and he gave it to Millar to bring him in sweets and buns.

The bell rang. It was lunch-time. The boarders gathered round the refectory door while the day-boys swaggered past calling them 'hairies' and 'grubby boarders'.

Colm stood beside Chit, both of them watching with patient regret the day-boys running down the straight avenue, and out through the open gates. They could see an odd tram passing, and they envied the day-boys their freedom.

'It's as bad as the jail in here,' Chit squeaked, his hands in his pockets, his face ink-spotted.

'It won't be long now till the holidays. And then ...' Colm wagged his head with delight.

'Oh, Colm, boy,' said Chit, putting his arm round Colm's shoulder. 'When I get home I'll lie in bed till twelve o'clock in the day and have four fried eggs for my breakfast every morning. Do you like fried eggs?'

'Man, I do! They make your hair curly.'

They went into the refectory. It was cold. They sat down

at the long rows of tables with the wrinkled table cloths. The fellow who was pouring out the tea from the white enamel urn put his hands around it to get a heat.

'Hi, hi,' they shouted. 'Pour out the dishwater and don't freeze it.'

Outside, the wind skimmed along the playing fields, jumped at the windows, and washed the panes to a cold blue.

When they came out they stamped with their hands in their pockets up and down the long corridor. Colm and Chit stood near the door waiting for Millar. Soon he arrived, his chin sunk in the turned-up collar of his coat, and a muddied cap in his hand.

'It would skin a louse that day. And look at my cap. It blew off.'

'Did you get the things?' Colm asked.

Millar winked one eye and then the other. The three of them walked down the corridor, stole into the science room, and behind a bench they sat on the floor. Colm divided the buns and sweets.

'Only for the ould daffodils and the March winds we wouldn't have this,' Millar said.

Chit mumbled with his mouth full.

THREE

A week before the Easter holidays the fellows went around swaggering and pulling out everyone's tie. In the breaks between the classes they began singing:

> This day fortnight where will we be,
> Out of the gates of misery . . .

Colm didn't join much in the jollity. Day after day he waited longingly for a letter with money to take him home. And then three days before the break-up he almost gave up hope. He had heard of fellows who had stayed on in the College for the Easter holidays, their parents wanting to save expense, and the fellows pretending that they'd rather stay than go home. He would have to make some excuse to Chit and Millar. But the arrival of a letter on the day before the holidays dissolved all his fears.

It was from his mother. He read it over and over again

with a mixture of joy and sorrow; they were all leaving the island for Belfast: Alec had got his job back in the bakery, and, as Theresa couldn't get off, he would call for Colm to get the house ready. He put the letter in his pocket. It was the end of being a boarder anyway. He kicked a pebble going round the track, and when Chit and Millar saw him approach they shouted, 'Here comes the good MacNeill.' Colm stopped, pulled out their ties, and raced with joy round the track with Chit and Millar chasing him.

The next day Alec came for him and together they went in the tram to their new house. It was in the middle of a street of little red-bricked houses. There were two bedrooms, and downstairs a kitchen and a parlour. When they opened the back door they looked out upon a large stretch of waste ground: clothes-lines hung here and there; hens moved about; and boys were playing football, bundles of coats marking the goal-posts. Opposite was a long black paling enclosing private grounds ringed with trees, and on the paling someone had scrawled in white letters: UP THE REBELS; REMEMBER 1916. At the top of the street were the brickyard and brickfields, and beyond that again more fields straggling up to the foot of a mountain. The mountain was so close they could see a few scattered houses at its foot and cattle in the fields.

Alec made up his mind to take Colm and Jamesy over the mountain and show them Lough Neagh, Belfast with its long tongue of a lough, and if the day was clear they'd see the hills of Galloway in Scotland. But Colm was disappointed when he was told that they wouldn't be able to see Knocklayde.

When they came in Colm wandered about the bare house. The walls were dotted with nails and where pictures had hung were square marks like sunlight. Between the floor boards match-heads and candle grease were stuck and in one place Colm saw a half-penny. He tried to lift it out with a pin, then he pulled the boards apart to get his fingers between them. His two fingers were on it when it slipped and fell. He got up from his knees. From the bedroom window he watched the boys playing football, and heard them shouting, 'Our out!' whenever the ball hit the paling.

Downstairs Alec was whistling and it sounded loud and deafening in the empty house. A cockroach raced across the red tiles towards the coal-house and Alec cracked it with his boot: 'I hope there's not many of them boyos about. The smell of them would knock you down.'

They went out together, Alec to the station to collect the things they had taken from the island, Colm to Smithfield where Alec had bought second-hand furniture. Later in the evening they would both go to meet their mother, Jamesy, and Clare.

At Smithfield Colm helped the man to lift the furniture on to the empty coal-van: a yellow arm-chair, a black sofa with a spring bulging out of the bottom, a little bamboo table, a chest of drawers, and a deal table. When it was all safely on top, the man sat on the arm-chair in front of the van, reins in hand and a cigarette in his mouth. Colm sat at the back, one hand holding the bamboo table. They set off along King Street and turned on to the Falls Road. Boys at street corners laughed and joked at the man driving from the arm-chair. At Hughes and Dickson's Flour Mill Colm saw, through an open door, steel hand-rails and a man naked to the waist feeding a furnace, but when he raised his eyes to the top of the high building his head got dizzy, and he turned his head away until the cart had passed. All the narrow cobbled streets were filled with playing children. A man was writing on a shop window: EGGS DOWN AGAIN. In a doorway a woman with a shawl over her head blew her nose in the tail of her skirt. A tram passed with a little boy clinging on to the lamp.

When the mill horns screeched loudly girls in their bare

feet and black slips with scissors dangling from a strap came flowing out of the doors. They were pale-faced and there was a smell of tow and oil off them. The driver winked at them and they shouted back. Then four girls passed linked together, swinging their tea-cans and laughing.

'Aw, Lizzie, luck at Lord Alphonsus!'

'Hello, daughters,' answered the driver. 'Do you want a lift?'

The driver slowed down and Colm blushed when he saw the four mill-doffers running towards the back of the van. They hopped up, two to each side of him, their faces smeared with dirt and pouse in their hair.

'All aboard, ladies ... Gee up, Suzina!' the driver shouts at the horse, cocking his cap to the side of his head, and holding the whip as straight as a flag-pole.

'That's a quare nice wee fella!' says one of the girls.

'Are you the Duke's son?" says another, and snuffled loudly.

Colm didn't answer and the cart rattled and bumped over the hard road.

'Is that yer da?' says another.

'Ah, Mary, lave him alone; he's my boy. Aren't you, dearie?'

At that moment one of the wheels came off and girls, furniture, and all slid off in a bundle on to the road. Fellows cheered. But when the trams came up and clanged their bells for the cart to move off, and it on its three wheels, Colm was so ashamed that he stood afar off pretending that he didn't belong to the annoyance.

He was glad when he was back in his own street again. They were waiting for Alec to come with the key when a young boy offered to get his mother's key to open the door. He called himself John Burns. He helped to carry in the furniture and later brought Colm up to his house where his mother gave him a mug of tea and a bap.

When Alec arrived with the island furniture Colm had a few boys around him. They helped to carry in the pictures, the rolled-up mattresses, his mother's sewing-machine, a crock filled with delft, a wooden trunk, a statue of the Sacred Heart in a glass cover, and a few odds and ends.

Later they went to the station. The evening still held its light when the train came in.

Standing outside the ticket-barrier they saw their mother approach in a black plush coat and black hat, Clare holding on to her hand, and behind them Jamesy in grey knickerbockers and Rover on a rope jumping round him.

Alec and Colm had great welcome for them, and they passed out of the station, Jamesy and Colm together and the dog licking them and tossing its head with delight.

'He knows him, mother. Look, mother, he knows Colm!'

'He'd be a stupid dog if he didn't,' said Alec.

The noise of the city traffic made the dog squirm with fright, and Jamesy lifted him in his arms as they went into a tram and sat downstairs. The boys talked loudly and the people stared at them. They exchanged news, Colm of the street and Jamesy about the island, Uncle Robert, Paddy John Beg, and Father Byrne. Rover put his nose under Jamesy's coat and Clare held tightly to the seat of the tram.

Back in the house it was dark; Alec hadn't remembered to go down to the Gas Office to have the gas turned on and they had to move about by candle light and pin newspapers across the bare windows to keep the neighbours from looking in. It was chilly, and to take the frost out of the air and to boil the kettle Alec lit a fire of sticks and old felt that he had found in the bin.

They had to sleep on the mattresses on the floor and Rover was put into the yard, but he whined and barked so much that the mother came into the boys' room: 'Do you hear Rover, Alec? He's breaking his heart.'

As they listened, a man pushed down a window and

shouted, 'Take in that dog to hell out o' that.'

Then a woman yelled, 'Take in your neb and let the poor people get into the house in peace!'

Alec stood at the window and was about to pull it down when his mother caught him by the arm, 'Don't say anything, Alec. God only knows what kind of neighbours we've got. Just let Rover in for the one night; he finds the place strange, poor fellow.'

When the dog got in he raced up the stairs and across the bed on the floor, whining and mad with joy. Colm and Jamesy covered themselves up with the clothes, shuddering with delight as the dog ran over the humped blankets. He licked their faces and Colm hugged him and then Jamesy hugged him saying,

'Aw, let him sleep between us!'

'Let him sleep between us!' shouted Alec from the head of the bed. 'D'ye want to have the bed a nest of fleas? He's lucky to get into the house itself without yez making an hotel for him.'

And in the darkness each would whisper to the dog and Rover would sniff at the corners of the blankets, Colm putting out a finger to feel the wet nose. Alec shouted to the dog to lie down and at last he went to a corner of the room and lay on a few newspapers.

When all was still again Colm stretched out his hand quietly and Rover sniffed at it and ran over the blankets.

'Now who's eggin' on that dog?' said Alec. 'It's you, Colm ... Lie down there, Rover, and don't budge or out you and Colm will go to the yard.'

There was peace after that and listening now to the groan of the last trams racing for the depot they fell into a deep sleep.

FOUR

Colm and Jamesy were not long in making friends. Boys gathered around the house, calling in at the back-door: 'Is Colm in, Mrs MacNeill?' or 'Is Jamesy coming up the fields?'

They got to know them quickly. They all had nicknames: Sheriff McCann – because he was always talking about cowboys; Croppy Caulfield – because his mother always clipped his hair like a jail-bird; Cheater Brennan and Clute Toner. They had a football team – 'Brickfield Star' – and Colm and Jamesy joined it.

At night when the big people were home from work they went round the doors asking in nice quiet voices, 'Please subscribe to Brickfield Football Team.'

'How much are they giving?' a woman said, and they told her to look at the card. She brought it in to the light of the kitchen and read with dubious astonishment:

Mrs Rogan 1/-
Mr Maguire 6d
Mrs Tully 6d

The boys at the door winked knowingly when they heard the chink of money. When the woman came to the door she handed them the card and twopence:

'Let that be the last of your football for a long time, for I'm tired subscribing.'

Once away from the house they gave the card to Colm, because he was the neatest handwriter, to put the woman's name down for sixpence.

'The higher subs you put down the more the people will give you,' John Burns said.

Then to the next house and when the woman refused to subscribe they mumbled amongst themselves:

'Aw, I always knew she was an ould miser! We'll bap her door tonight, boys!'

On Saturday the committee went down town to buy the new ball, going from one shop to another until they were satisfied where the best bargain was to be had. Each took turns at carrying the ball as they marched proudly home, eating sweets bought with the few pence that were left over. They began to run when they came in sight of the street and saw the rest of the team rubbing their hands and racing to meet them. They crowded round the new ball exclaiming with delight: 'She's a dinger!'; 'She's as hard as iron!'

Out on the waste ground at the back of the street they picked sides and played all the evening.

The following Saturday they challenged a Protestant team to a match in the Bog Meadows. Heaps of stones were used for goal-posts, and when Jamesy sent in a shot that just passed over the goalkeeper's head a dispute arose. Brickfield Star said it was a good goal, but the other team maintained that

the ball went over the 'bar'. The match finished in a fight.
The Protestants began to sing:

> O Dolly's Brae, O Dolly's Brae,
> O Dolly's Brae no more,
> For the tune we'll play is
> Kick the Pope
> Right over Dolly's Brae.

A burst of cheering and booing marked the end of the song.
Showers of stones were exchanged and then Brickfield Star
began to sing:

> Soldiers are we
> Whose lives are pledged to Ireland . . .

When they reached the end of it they shouted 'Rickey
Charge!' and chased the Prods from the ground, but they
soon returned with reinforcements and Brickfield retreated
shouting and waving their fists: 'Wait till we get you on
our ground' – glad to have the satisfaction of threatening
though they knew that they would never meet that team
again.

When the evenings lengthened they played amongst
themselves on the waste ground, the sweat breaking out on
them, running across to the scullery for drinks of cold water,
and then out again filled with a fresh new joy.

Sometimes Alec watched them, smiling at Jamesy in goal
and pieces of his old drawers cut up and made into knee-caps.
Tired, he turned and went to his pigeon shed, built on the
low slates overlooking the yard. He had a ladder up to it
and he loved to come in of an evening when the pigeons
were roosting and the air thick with heat and the smell of
meal. He would scrape out the shed, spread new corn for
them, and fill the drinking troughs with fresh water. Under
the light of a candle he would take down his favourite birds

from the roosts, stroke them softly with the palm of his hand, and put them back again. He loved to see them pairing together and nesting, and sometimes when he came home from work he would begin to make new trap–doors and nest-boxes.

Colm took no interest in the pigeons, and on Saturday night when Alec and Jamesy went down town to talk with the bird-fanciers who congregated in Gresham Street, Colm went off by himself around the stalls in Smithfield, looking at the second-hand books, listening to the gramophones and watching a man making keys while-you-wait. Then to the clothes stall where blankets, coloured quilts, women's coats, men's swallow-tails, hung from the rafters overhead making the place cool and dark.

A woman sits on a stool with her hat and coat on and holds up a shirt as people pass: 'Mister, a bargain for one-and-six! . . . Here it is for a bob! He doesn't want it . . . H'm, collar and tie and all included he wants! . . . What have we here! Yes, that's the very I-T. A dress shirt, ready to wear, as stiff as a corpse! . . . How much! Don't all rush. Ninepence to you, sir! You never know the day you are going to get married. He doesn't want it neither. Gold cuff links and all he wants . . . The people nowadays want no one to live.'

At another stall two shawled women were bargaining over a roll of oil–cloth, and near them in a side passage were tables, old golf clubs, fire irons, coal-buckets, and a model yacht with its sails rolled up. Colm's heart went out to the yacht but when he asked the price, it was too dear, and his face got red as he told the stall owner that he would call back again. He passed out of Smithfield on to the street and stood to watch an old man with a monkey. The man had a handle–organ tied round his neck with pieces of cord. The monkey, dressed in a vest and trousers, held a cocoa tin with a slit cut in the lid and sometimes he shook it to let the spectators know that he wanted money.

A man with clogs on his feet and a tall hat on his head passed through the crowd selling *Old Moore's Almanac*, while his brother stood at the corner of Gresham Street selling corn plasters and people called him the Corn King. He, too, had a tall hat and round the sides of it were pieces of cardboard inscribed with red-inked letters: REMOVE THAT CORN.

At 9:30 Colm would go round to the bird-shop for Alec and Jamesy. Men and youths stood around in groups and the roadway was always covered with their spits. They held up pigeons in their hands under the street lamps trying to sell them for a sixpence or a shilling, and then when the crowd was breaking up for the night they would offer the birds for half the price.

The bird-shop windows were well-lighted and the songs of many birds came into the night air. White rabbits lay asleep in the window; ferrets were enclosed in wired boxes and gold fish scintillated under the lights. Colm often watched them until Alec and Jamesy were ready for home.

Then they would call into a chip-shop where Alec bought them chips and brought some wrapped in paper for his mother. Carrying parcels they would arrive home dead weary to find their mother bent over the table smoothing shirts and pinnies, for the next day was Sunday and she liked her children to go out clean to Mass.

It was always on Sunday that Theresa had an evening off and often she brought Joe Heaney up to the house, and her mother would have her best delft on the table and biscuits and currant bread for the tea. And then when they would go out again Colm and Jamesy would be snapping at the remaining biscuits on the plate and the mother scolding them: 'Ye'd think ye were starved and the dacent lad hardly gone from the door.'

They loved a Sunday for it meant a visit from Joe and a few pence each from him, and because it always gave them a day in the fields or a walk to the mountain. But when the summer holidays came they had six long weeks of glorious freedom.

When the sun was warming the bricks of the houses a crowd of boys in their bare feet would call for Colm and Jamesy, and with pieces of bread in their hands they would join them and set off for a swim at Toneroy.

They climbed through the cool fields where the buttercups yellowed their bare legs, stopping now and then to pull the grass from between their toes or to look back at the street and the brickyard falling far below them; out on to the country road with the tar bubbling on it under the sun, racing for a drink at the horse-trough, and then as they came in sight of the mountain pool they began to pull off their jerseys. Then they bathed in the black cold water, and ran nakedly up and down the fields, letting the wind and the sun dry them. They followed the river along cool glens and gathered blue bells with the sun caught in the net of leaves above their heads; after trout under stones; chased by the gamekeeper; up the fields again, panting madly, and so out on to the road again for home, their bodies cool from the bathe, stomachs empty from hunger, pockets empty of the few pence that would buy the dry loaf that would satisfy them. Some would break sticks and bite rings in them with their teeth, the sour taste scorching their mouths.

The smallest and most ragged boy amongst them would be sent up to the little farm-houses to beg and a fight would take place over the bread till the 'beggar' got none. They would splash dust over their legs to pretend they had walked for miles and miles, and then burst into song as the cool of the evening began to fall like dew and the lights of the city come out as slow as summer stars. Their voices would rise:

One man went to mow, went to mow a meadow;

One man and his dog went to mow a meadow.

and so on to:

> Twenty men went to mow, went to mow a
>   meadow;
> Twenty men, nineteen men, eighteen men . . .
> . . . three men, two men,
> One man and his dog went to mow a meadow.

till their throats were parched and their hearts full of joy. They would take the short cut through the fields now wet with dew, forgetting about the dust on their legs; and so in sight of the brickfield and their street with its lamps lit and a mist falling on the waste ground. They would sing again, knowing their mothers would be gossiping at the back-doors, anxious for their return.

Then they give wild Indian calls as they break into a run, their sticks rattling along the ribled edges of the tin palings. The mothers would smile and look up at the darkening fields, listening happily to the shouts of their boys.

'Here they come,' they'd say. 'They'll be dying with hunger.'

Fires would be poked, kettles boiled, and a clean newspaper spread on the table. And then home, sitting on the fender, re-telling the day's events, wiping the sweat from their faces with the lining of their caps, and then later to bed to lie awake for a minute and then to fall into a blessed sleep.

Towards the end of that summer when the holidays were nearly over Colm, Jamesy, and Clare went with their mother on the last excursion of the season to Bangor. It, too, was on a Sunday. Crowds of people waved the boat off as she swung out from the wooden pier, and sailed down the lough. Behind, the boat left a suddy path in the water; gulls' shadows skimmed across the deck; and far away now, tiny trams were sliding over Queen's Bridge.

The city lay spread out in a loop, Cave Hill and the Divis range at one side, and the field-patterned Castlereagh Hills at the other; and because it was Sunday there was little smoke from the tall factory chimneys, but below in a blue haze stretched parallel rows of red-bricked houses choking each other for space. High up on the slope of the Black Mountain Colm pointed out to Jamesy where Toneroy lay; and then as the boat passed the shipyards with the skeletons of ships seen through a net of scaffolding, they began to play hide-and-go-seek with Clare, and sometimes for devilment shouted down the ventilators. Then they lifted Clare in their arms to see the terrifying splendour of the ship's engine, but the stuffy smell of heat and oil dizzied her head and she went and sat beside her mother, running a finger over her plush coat, making dark wavy lines on the velvety surface, and smoothing them out again to see the lines mysteriously vanish.

Colm would call her to see a train on the shore waving a long twisted roll of smoke to them, or maybe far out on the blue sea a yacht, its sails swan-white in the sun. Then as they drew near Bangor the boom of a Salvation Army Band came to them over the quiet water. All the people crowded to one side, tilting the boat, and nearly putting the heart out of Clare and her mother. Colm and Jamesy laughed at them and they both leaned over the rails in an attempt to cant the boat a little more.

Out at Ballyholme they paddled in the water and screamed with joy. Colm would cover Clare's legs with sand, the cold taking her breath away, and she would call out, 'Look, Mammie, look! I've no legs!'

The mother bought them Bangor rock and Clare chewed hers quickly, fascinated by the name that never disappeared however much she ate.

And the mother sitting with her umbrella beside her

smiled happily, looking at the sun-winking waves breaking on the sand. And she'd smile again and shrug her shoulders as she'd hear the happy screams of her children: 'Aw, but it's a grand day, thank God,' and she'd join her hands on her lap, looking at a gull making a nest of rings for itself in the water.

Near them a few girls went in for a bathe and when Colm saw them he thought of Uncle Robert and Aunt Maggie and he repeated their remarks: 'Look at them bold heelers and not as much clothes on them as'd dust a flute.' His mother lifted her umbrella and made a clout at him.

Into a little café they went for tea, and Clare spilled hers on the white American cloth, but the mother scooped it into her cup again. And then out on their way to the boat; but Jamesy stopped to look at a toy yacht lying on the lawn of a house, and stuck his head so far between the railings that he couldn't get it out. Crowds gathered and a policeman came, and as the sawed iron sizzled around his neck it was then Jamesy began to cry and his eyes saw stars falling around them. Off they hurried with the sniffing Jamesy, but the boat was gone. The mother had just enough money to take them back on the train and they had to walk home, tired and cross through the deserted Sunday streets of Belfast.

Up along High Street they went, Colm seeing their reflections in the blinds of the big shop windows as they passed. They turned into the Falls Road. Here there was life. An ice-cream man was standing between the shafts of his barrow rattling the lid. Loads of children, returning from a day in the Park, were shouting from the tops of trams; boys held aloft empty bottles that had held watery milk, the girls waved rags of handkerchiefs, all their faces smeared from the jammed pieces devoured in the cool of the trees. But the MacNeills were too tired, too cross, for their hearts to leap with joy, Clare alone of them envious and lagging behind. Then she'd run and, catching up with them say, her voice quivering with vexation, 'Take the tram, Mammie. Take the tram. I'm tired.' They paid no heed to her as they trudged on with the sweat breaking on them.

Away in front the sun was sinking behind Divis, its evening light flowing into the tram lines and dusting with gold the sooty spires of St Peter's. Around them the mills were strangely silent, the flock on the wire-guarded windows disturbed by no draught, the brick walls oozing out the heat held captive during the day.

'Och, such a day,' would come from the mother, as she dragged her feet. 'To think that twopence ha'penny would take us home in comfort and me without a fluke!'

And when she got into the house she stirred up the fire under the kettle, made tea, and sent Colm off to bed early as he had to rise for school in the morning.

FIVE

'What are you writing?' said Colm to Jamesy when he came in one evening to do his homework and saw the leaves of an exercise scattered over the table. The kitchen was empty and the gas lit.

'I'm writing to Uncle Robert. He told me to write him a long letter about all the neighbours in the street.'

Colm lifted some of the sheets and began to read:

Dear Uncle Robert

We are all well. Theresa is getting married soon and is going to live in Birmingham and we'll have great sport. The holidays are over and Colm has to do six exercises and he learns French. I was on the altar but got put off for not rising early in the mornings. Clare is in the fourth book and Alec has fifteen pigeons and he brings them in a basket on the bar of his bicycle and lets them off at Lisburn. I am getting a job soon in

McGrath's Grocery running messages, and if I do well I'll get behind the counter. I am going to tell you about the people in the street on sheets of paper. I hope you and Aunt Maggie are well.

From,
Jamesy

The first house is the wee shop and Mrs McGonigle lives here. She has an orchard in Glenavy and every Saturday her husband goes up and gets two bags of apples to make candy apples. She keeps two collie dogs and every Friday she sends down to the chip-shop for a fish with no vinegar for each of the dogs. She is a miser and gives you bad value in your sweets.

No. 3 is Mrs Kelly an old cross lady with two sons in America. She was going to send the peelers on us for lighting the bonfire on the 15th August facing her door. We never hardly see her.

No. 5 is Colonel Magee and he works in the post office. He is very rich and he has a new bicycle and curls in his moustache. He walks as straight as a lamp-post and he fought in the Boer War. He has a sword in the kitchen and he always cleans it with Brasso and he gave us a shilling for our football club. His wife keeps flowers in the yard and he has two larks in a cage. On a Sunday he wears a hard hat and goes for a walk up the road with his wee black pom.

No. 7 lives Biddy McAteer, one of the queerest people in the street. Her door is hardly ever opened. She lives with her 3 brothers and her father. Tony works in the laundry in a cart and at dinner time he leaves the horse and cart outside the door for about an hour. Sometimes the horse gets tired standing and walks down the street. They have planks on top of the shed in the yard and because we tried to steal them for our bonfire Joe nailed them together. Biddy never washes the windows and they are as black as a nigger.

No. 9 is Mrs Tully and she is the kindest woman in the street. If she sent you up to the wee shop a message she'd give you a penny or an orange. All the children like to go her messages. She has two big sons and three daughters. One of her sons is working in London in a good job and the other big one cleans out the carriages in the railway, and he always comes home with bundles of newspapers in all his pockets. Her young son is spoiled and gets everything he wants. He has crowds of toys which he doesn't use and if his mother gave one away he would start to cry.

No. 11 is Da McVeigh and his wife died a month ago and he sits in the dark and never lights the gas.

No. 13 lives Mrs O'Brien a good living woman that goes to Mass every morning. Her daughter collects for the black babies on Sunday. She was stopped by two policemen who asked her if she was collecting for some secret society. She told them that she was collecting for the black pagans in Africa and they walked away.

No. 15 is where we live.

No. 17 is Mrs Hamill. She lives with her daughter and the two of them are deaf. It would make you laugh if you heard the two of them talking to each other. They talk so loud that you would think they were fighting. The only one they speak to is my mother.

No. 19 is where Mr Burns lives and he works at the docks and comes home covered with flour. He always chalks tips for the races when he goes out early to his work. He has a canary and he brings it out to the yard and it will fly round and round and light on the clothes line and then go into the cage again. His son,

John, is a chum of mine and Colm's and his father beats him if he doesn't wash the yard. He mitches from school and the schoolboard has it in for him. His sister has a notion of our Alec.

I don't know much about the people in Nos 21, 23, 25.

No. 27 is the end house on this side of the street and the man works in the brickyard and his clothes and boots are the colour of the clay. He goes to the football matches to see Celtic and if they win he comes home drunk and he would give you a penny. He hunts us if we play handball against the gable. His son keeps a whippet and he feeds it on tripe and it runs in the races but it never wins. He walks it every day on a lead and it has a brown coat on it in the cold days.

'What are you going to do now?' asked Colm, when he had finished reading the sheets.

'Write about the other side of the street,' Jamesy replied.

'You'll waste no more of my paper and anyway I want the pen to do my exercises.'

Jamesy gave him the pen and held the last written sheet near the bars of the grate to dry. The paper scorched and he made a face at the yellow stain. Then he folded the sheets together and got Colm to address the envelope.

'You've ruined the nib,' he said crossly. 'With your ould scraggy writing, you can get a pen of your own the next time.'

Jamesy whistled. 'We're not all smarties like yourself.'

'G-r-r-r –' said Colm angrily as Jamesy raced out the door.

He ruled his exercise neatly with red ink and was ready to begin when his mother and Theresa came in laden with parcels in preparation for the wedding. They began to chatter, and in disgust Colm threw down the pen and banged the door after him as he went out.

SIX

It was a Saturday morning in September, Theresa's wedding day. The mother had been moving about the house since daybreak. Alec and Colm were early awake, and Clare had brought up the morning's paper for Alec to read in bed. Colm lay beside him and at the foot of the bed was Jamesy sleeping through the stir.

'He could sleep on a clothes-line, that fellow,' said Alec. 'I wish to God I was like him.'

When they got out of bed Colm and Jamesy put on new grey suits, black stockings and new boots. Colm plastered his fair hair with water. Jamesy had used some of Alec's hair oil the night before, and now that it had dried in, his hair stuck up straight and he couldn't press it down.

The mother made a fuss about every little thing: she made Jamesy take off his boots and lace them over again because he had missed two holes. Alec was to do best man and whilst shaving he cut himself and put blood on the only stiff collar that he had. His mother said it was awful looking and to please her he scraped the blood off with a knife and rubbed the soiled part with bread crumbs.

'I'll do all right,' he said. 'Nobody'll be looking at me; all eyes on the bride, Theresa – eh,' and he hit himself on the chest and strode up and down the kitchen.

Theresa was too busy to listen to him. She had her mouth full of hair-pins and her small pink hat lay on the table. She wore a pair of brown suede shoes and a pink dress down to her heels.

'I'm a holy show,' she whimpered into the square looking-glass on the wall. 'My hair's cut too short. Them hair-dressers'll do nothing you tell them!'

'I never seen you looking better in my life; you're gorgeous, child,' placated the mother. 'I hope you're warm enough; it wouldn't suit you to get a cold on your wedding day. Have you yer heavy chemise on?'

Theresa wasn't listening. 'Is that bow at the back all right, Gertie?' she was saying to Gertie Tully, the bridesmaid. 'I'll faint before I reach the chapel.'

Colm sat on the sofa, weak with excitement, the morning's paper in his hand which he hadn't the heart to read while Jamesy kept running in and out saying, 'The motor's not in sight yet!' and always the mother replied, 'Stay outside till it comes and give my head peace!'

'Oh, where did I leave the comb! Mother! Did you see the comb?' Theresa's voice quivered with nervousness.

Gertie Tully looked for it in the scullery, Colm looked on the mantelpiece, and Theresa lifted and flung the clothes from the sewing-machine: 'Such a house and only one comb in it!'

'Here it is!' said the mother, finding it in her apron pocket. 'Don't fuss, child. Take it easy!'

'Are you sure that clock's right, Mother?' said Theresa, looking up at the clock on the mantelpiece. 'Run out,

Colm, and get the time from Mrs McGonigle; she always has it right.'

As Colm got up to go Jamesy came running in, 'Here's the taxi, Theresa. Here's the motor!'

'Oh! and me only half ready!'

'Take yer time, daughter. He's getting good money and he can wait a wheen of minutes.'

The buzz of children's voices and the purr of the motor came in through the open door.

Alec brought the driver into the scullery for 'a mouthful' and the wee fellows outside began bamping the horn – adding to the buzz, the excitement, and the confusion.

'Go out, Colm,' shouted Alec, 'and give them cheeky warts a scud on the lug!'

When all was ready and they were going out the door the mother called Alec back. She had noticed a scrap of white thread on his coat where the shop-ticket had not been carefully removed. She snipped it with the scissors, Alec standing impatient as a young foal, listening to the commotion. 'You'll have me as excited as yourself if you keep on the way yer doing,' he said.

She pulled his coat down and brushed his shoulders with her hand. 'You'll do now, son,' and she pushed him out in front of her.

All the children and neighbours were in the street, and someone had tied two brickyard-men's boots to the back of the taxi and chalked up – DOUBLE TRAGEDY.

They moved to the side as Gertie Tully, in blue, and Theresa, in pink, came out of the house.

'She looks lovely, God love her,' a neighbour said.

'She's getting a nice tidy wee lump of a man, anyway,' from another.

'Isn't she a picture, the creature.'

Boys stood on window-sills and one had climbed a lamp-post to get a better view, and then as the motor moved off they began to cheer, and Rover went barking after it down the street. Colm and Jamesy were left behind with Mrs Burns and Mrs Tully who were going to make the breakfast.

In the taxi Alec sat with the driver, Clare on her mother's knee, and one big seat was given to Theresa and Gertie so that their dresses would not be crushed. The mother had a handkerchief in her hands, and whenever she felt a tear rising she would look up at the roof of the car or turn away from Theresa's gaze.

Theresa rubbed her hands and said in almost a whisper, 'I wish this was over!'

'I only wish it was my day,' added Gertie. 'God only knows I might be left on the shelf!'

They all gave a forced laugh and remained silent.

In the house Colm and Jamesy were looking at the scullery crammed with parcels: bread, cake, jamrolls, boxes of pastry, and a box of paper hats, toy balloons, and squeakers. On the floor were rows of black porter bottles with brown labels, and in a basket bottles of lemonade.

'We're going to have some spree the day,' said Jamesy, giving a little dance. 'I wish we had a few more sisters.'

'It'll be like Christmas,' added Colm.

Mrs Burns came into the scullery to get the pan. 'I'll give you two boys your breakfast and get you out of the road.'

She fried them sausages, ham, an egg each, and potato bread. And everything was cleared away when the motor came back from the chapel, and Colm and Jamesy raced for their packets of rice to shower on Theresa and Joe. Joe gave them a half-crown each, and they bought sweets, went to the matinee in Clonard Picture House, and hurried back again for the evening's sport.

The house was crowded and there were men and women there whom they did not know. Theresa had on a new dress, a paper hat on her head, and Joe was heading a balloon. The kitchen and parlour were filled with smoke, and the table was laid for the tea. Now and again Alec would burst a balloon.

Joe's mother was sitting on the sofa, swaying backwards and forwards. She was a little fat woman with two broad rings on one finger, and her squeaky voice could be heard above the chatter, 'Och, och. Now, now!' She gave Jamesy sixpence to sing the 'Turf Man from Ardee', and when he stood up, Alec put a chair in the middle of the floor and made him stand on it.

Jamesy held the sixpence in his fist and he nearly forgot the words as he thought of what he would buy with it. At the end of the second verse he wondered why they all giggled:

> Your cart is wrecked and worn, friend,
> Your ass is very old,
> It must be twenty summers
> Since that animal was foaled.

> 'He was yoked in a trap when I was born,
> September, forty-three,
> And he cantered for the mid-wife,'
> Said the turf-man from Ardee.

> 'I often do abuse the beast with this rough hazel
>   rod,
> Although, I owe, I never yet
> Drive poor old Jack, unshod.
> The harness now that's on his back
> Was made by John Magee,
> Who's dead this two and forty years,'
> Said the turf-man from Ardee.

They clapped wildly at the end of the song, and Jamesy ran out for fear they would ask him to sing again. Later he came back and stole pieces of cake and a bottle of lemonade for

John Burns and Croppy Caulfield. They had to break the neck of the bottle to get it opened and use a cocoa tin as a tumbler. John Burns said that he was the decentest fellow that ever was and if his sister got married he would smuggle out a bottle for Jamesy.

Alec played the melodeon, somebody a mouth organ and a mandolin. Everyone was asked to sing and afterwards they played 'forfeits'. Colm slipped out when he heard about the forfeits and went up to the pigeon-shed and sat in the dark, looking down into the kitchen at the coloured balloons above all the heads of the people.

A hat was filled with all the collected 'forfeits': a watch, bangles, powder-puffs, combs, pencils, and Jamesy's sixpence. Alec was the 'dreamer'.

The first forfeit that was held up was a man's watch.

'What has this young man to do?' Alec was asked, and he blind-folded.

'He has to take off his right boot and dance around saying, "I'm a fool! I'm a fool!" '

The man stooped to take off his boot and everyone roared when they saw his big toe sticking out through his stocking.

'He needs a wife anyway,' Joe said.

The next forfeit was Jamesy's sixpence, and he was told to put out the lamp at the other side of the street and to light it again.

Jamesy crossed the street, twined his legs round the lamp and speeled up with two matches in his teeth. He put his hand on the screw and turned it; the lamp went out. He caught one of the horizontal bars, struck a match, and lit the lamp again. They clapped him when he came back. His face was red and his blue eyes shining. Two girls tried to kiss him, but he struggled free and when Theresa and Joe were leaving for the Fleetwood boat Jamesy was nowhere to be found.

The boat was to leave at ten o'clock and Alec and Colm carried the bags. Clare with a black and white muffler round her neck went with her mother and Mrs Heaney. Jamesy had seen them go and as soon as they were out of sight he slipped into the house, gathered all the empty porter bottles in a basket, and sold them in a pub for fourteen pence.

At the boat it was cold and dark. Warm lights here and there zig-zagged in the black water and a draughty breeze blew up from the lough. Some soldiers were on deck shouting at girls on the quay. Joe and Theresa leaned over the rail, a dreary light shining on them. Joe was joking, but there were tears in Theresa's eyes. Colm was watching the soldiers, and then when he saw through a port-hole into the lighted interior a desire for the sea rushed over him.

When the boat hooted Clare jumped and caught her mother by the arm. The engines started and the water swirled from the stern and clopped stormily against the quay. They waved and waved until they could see nothing only a boat with lines of lighted port-holes.

'God knows we might never see them again. They grow up and they leave you!'

'Och, Mother, I'm surprised at you talking like that,' said Alec. 'You'd think they were going to Australia to hear you! And him going to his good job in Birmingham!'

The two mothers were crying. Colm yawned when he felt a catch in his throat and he turned his back and looked towards the curve of lights on Queen's Bridge. There was always a sadness in trains or boats going away, even when you had no friends leaving.

On the boat deck Theresa and Joe stood in a sheltering darkness. Theresa was crying. He kissed her and took her in his arms.

'Don't be crying, Theresa. Sure we have each other and nothing else matters!'

They stood for a long time close together. They watched the lights of Belfast diminish in a clump behind them, the lonely ruffled lights on both sides of the lough, and the glow in the sky above Bangor. Then the Copeland light shone clear in the darkness and suddenly everything was cold. They shivered and went below.

The place was cobwebbed with smoke. A young girl awakened from sleep smiled stupidly at them. Soldiers were lying with their caps off and great-coats buttoned around them. A man with his boots loosed lay with one hand touching the floor, a dribbling porter bottle lying on its side near him.

Joe took Theresa into a corner, made her stretch out, threw a coat over her legs, and taking her head on his lap, tried to sleep.

SEVEN

'It's a cold you've got at the boat. It'll go away in a few days.'

Colm's mother put warm olive oil into his ear and told him to turn in and sleep. But sleep he couldn't for his ear buzzed and jagged through the long night. At times he prayed and cried silently, trying not to waken Alec and Jamesy.

In the morning the pain had gone, but before going to school his mother brought him to the Monastery to have the relic applied to his ear. Coming out they called in the chapel, lit a candle, and while his mother did the Stations Colm knelt beside a statue of Saint Anthony, looking at the Child Jesus standing on an open book in the saint's arm. Colm couldn't pray; his mind was fuzzy, and all the time he kept wishing that his mother would hurry up and not keep him late for school. Presently she came and sat beside him and told him to say a few prayers for his father's soul. And then they got up to go. Passing down the narrow aisle in front of them was a woman with a child in each hand, and Colm had to lag behind them and wait at the holy water font until the woman had helped each of the children to make the sign of the cross.

Once outside the chapel he began to run, but he was late. The whole school day dragged and jangled.

On his way home he called in the Falls Road Library for a book of Irish History for Alec and it was nearly five o'clock when he arrived home. He hung his bag and cap on the knob of the banisters and went into the kitchen. He was tired and lay on the sofa.

His mother came in from the yard, crumpled clothes in her arms, and her apron pocket full of clothes-pegs.

'That was a grand drying day,' she said to herself, and turning round she saw Colm. 'Oh, what kept you? How's your ear?'

'It's all right now, Mother; I don't feel it.'

'Run up to the butcher's like a good boy and get a pound of liver for Alec's dinner.'

'Och, Mother, I'm tired. Anyway, I'm always running messages like a wee girl. Send Clare.'

'Do you want the child to get run over! Go on when you're bid; Alec'll be here any minute now.'

'No! I'm not going. You can get somebody out in the streets to go.'

'All right, don't go, just wait till Alec comes home and you'll sing "Sorry am I." '

Clare came running in by the back-door. 'Here's Alec, Mother. Here's Alec!'

'Will you go now?' said his mother.

Colm got up from the sofa sulkily. Alec knocked the flour off his cap against the yard-wall.

'It was sickening working in that bake-house this day,' he said when he came in.

'There's a fellow there that wouldn't go for liver for your dinner and he gave me back lip,' and seeing the look in Alec's eyes she lied quickly. 'But you needn't hit him. I gave him a couple of good thumps already.'

'Man, boy, if you don't obey your mother I'll break every bone in your body! Do you hear that?'

'Give me the money and I'll go!'

'You needn't bother yourself. I'm tired of liver anyway.'

'Will he get mince or sausages then?'

'I don't want a fry. I'll just take a mouthful of tea.'

Alec went into the scullery to wash himself and as the tap splashed over his hands he burst into the first verse of 'Nelly Deane'.

The mother whispered to Colm, 'Run down, son, and get a half-pound of cheese, and there's a penny for yourself. Not a word to Jamesy, now!'

He went out by the back-door and down to the shop at the foot of the street. He hated disobeying his mother but, anyway, he was getting big now and she shouldn't ask him to run the messages. When he came back Alec was standing in the middle of the floor drying his face in a towel and his mother had spread a clean newspaper on the table.

Jamesy came in, a blood-stained rag twisted round his finger.

'What's up with your finger?' asked the mother.

'I got it cut going over McCrae's palings for chestnuts. It's only a scratch.'

'There's always something happening since you got put off the altar. I don't know what has come over this house with sore ears and now sore fingers. Here's your tea and when the two of you get it, off you pop to Holy Family and get God's grace about you.'

After the tea Jamesy took possession of the sink in the scullery and Colm tried to do his exercises at the table.

'Wash behind your ears,' the mother was shouting in to

Jamesy. 'Brush the heels of your boots and don't be telling me that good soldiers never look behind.'

When the quarter-to-eight bells were ringing Colm and Jamesy went out to their Holy Family. At the bottom of the street Jamesy had to turn back as he had forgotten his prayer beads.

The streets were filled with a frosty October mist and the bells tolled loudly above the roofs of the houses. Boys came in groups from different streets and when they passed under a lamp-post the light glistened on their polished boots and water-plastered hair. They were all talking at once, and now and again two or three lingered behind to swap cigarette cards or play chestnuts.

Colm and Jamesy with their hands in their pockets took the short cut over the fields, past the dark brickyard, up a few narrow streets, and when they came to the Monastery Father Carthy was on the lighted porch, clapping his hands and urging the boys to hurry up. Colm and Jamesy went to their section – Our Lady of Sorrows. The prefect asked Jamesy why he was absent the last two meetings and he replied that he was sick.

The church was heated and boys were warming their hands on the hot pipes. Around the High Altar a misty incense had gathered from the October devotions just ended. Lights shone on the varnished seats and late boys raced to their places.

A priest ascended the pulpit and thumped it with his two fists. 'Silence!' he shouted. 'You'd think you were in a picture hall and not in the House of God! You wouldn't get boys from the Shankill Road to behave like you. The next boy I get talking, I'll run him out the door.'

The buzz dwindled and faded away. The priest dabbed his forehead with a handkerchief and then in a solemn tone gave out the Rosary. At the end of the prayers they all stood up and sang 'Happy We Who Thus United'.

An old priest then came into the pulpit and when he said that he'd tell stories the boys sat up in their seats with rigid attention.

'There was living at one time, my dear boys, in the heart of France, a little boy named Jacques. He was seven years of age, and it came to pass that this little boy was about to make his First Holy Communion. At school the master asked his First Communicants to write down on a sheet of paper the resolution they were going to make.

'What resolution did Jacques make, my dear boys! Listen! Listen! Are you all listening now? He wrote down that he would wear a white neck-tie when he was in the State of Grace. Now wasn't that a lovely thing for a boy so young?'

'Yes, Father,' they chorused.

'Ah, my dear little boys,' the priest continued, 'that indeed was a lovely thought! I wonder how many of you would even think of that! But that's not all. Our little friend grew up, left school, and became a soldier in the army of France.

'Day by day he was seen with his white neck-tie, an ever-present witness of the whiteness of the boy's soul – a soul never soiled by sin. Ah, my dear little boys, if we were only half as good as Jacques, how lovely and pure we would all be! As pure as the little birds in the air, the clouds in the sky, and the flowers in the field!

'Then one day our little friend was wounded in the battlefield. He lay on the ground and his heart's blood was slowly ebbing away and he began to pray. And then a priest was going around hearing the confessions of the dying and wounded, and soon he came to Jacques. The priest looked at the pure, shining eyes of our friend and he knew that he was in the presence of a saint.

' "Father," Jacques said, "When I was a young boy at school I made a promise that I would wear a white neck-tie until I committed a mortal sin, and here it is yet."

'So the priest sent the white neck-tie home to Jacques'

mother and Jacques died and his shining soul went radiantly up to Heaven.'

The boys began to talk and fidget at the end of the story, but the priest clapped his hands gently. Then he exhorted them to keep away from sin, from bad companions, and to follow Jacques' example.

The boys began to cough and grow restless, and the priest started another story. He told about a young boy called Michael Dawson who was going to be a jockey. Every night when at his prayers his companions threw pillows at him and hissed and catcalled. Then one night Michael went down to the stable, locked the door, knelt in the straw beside his horse and said his prayers. His friends started to giggle at him through the key-hole, but at last they got tired of it and in future they began to follow Michael Dawson's example of saying their prayers every night.

'Now, my dear young men, you see the power one good boy has over his companions. Be good always! Won't you? Be manly always! Say your prayers morning and night! Won't you do that, my dear boys?'

'Yes, Father!'

'If you do that, God will reward you ... God bless you all!' and giving the boys his blessing the old priest walked down from the pulpit.

The candles on the altar were now lighted for Benediction, and the organ began to play 'Tantum Ergo', the boys yelling the first line, fading away because they did not know the next words, and then bursting in again at *Genetori genetoque*, trailing off again leaving the rest to the choir and the organ until they reached the *Ame-e-e-e-n!*

Then silence as the Monstrance is raised above their bowed heads, the bell ringing, and the boys thumping their breasts. A pause, the chant of the *Divine Praises*:

Blessed be God.

Blessed be His holy Name . . .

and Benediction is over. They stand up to sing 'Faith of Our Fathers' and then out, rushing into the street, shouting, heel tripping, and calling their companions.

Colm and Jamesy went home together, down the cobbled streets, the lights now in all the windows, gramophones playing, and here and there the shadow of a bird-cage on the blind. Colm was quiet and Jamesy asked him what he was huffing about walking along like a dummy's meeting.

'If you want to know, Smarty, my ear is throbbing and I want a bit of peace.'

Silently they went across the fields, past the brickyard, seeing in the dark a stray donkey or a horse standing in the heat of the kilns. And then home, Colm to do more exercises, and Jamesy, because he had now left school, free to hammer at boxes in the yard or to take Rover out for a run before bed-time.

EIGHT

All the next day the pain in Colm's ear was intense. His mother kept him in bed, and now and again he cried out as the pain tore through his ear like a hot wire. Alec went for the doctor and Colm was ordered to the hospital.

That night he heard from his bed a motor creak to a standstill outside the house. Someone ascended the stairs and a nurse came into the room with a blanket over her arm. Alec wrapped him in the blanket and carried him downstairs. In a glance he saw Clare crying in the kitchen, a tired expression from his mother, and a melancholy smile on Jamesy's face. The door was crowded with boys, and John Burns said aloud, 'Here he is now!' But they were all quiet and gaping at Colm as he was put into the stretcher-bed at the back of the long car.

The oily smell of the exhaust thickened the rainy air and made Colm sick. But when the driver closed the back of the car the sickish smell was shut out, and Colm stared at the dim electric bulb and the blue glass window above the nurse's head. She put a cold hand on his forehead and it smelt of iodine. Lights passed in the blue window and the tyres fizzed on the wet road.

The nurse was young and began to read a letter. When she had finished she put her hand on his head again. 'You'll be all right soon. There's nothing much the matter with you. You'll be all right,' and she looked at the letter again and sighed loudly.

A big dark building stood before them, and the nurse put a pair of slippers on his feet and helped him up the stone steps. The inside of the hospital was aglow with light, and at the bottom of the stairs two nurses were talking. Up these Colm and the young nurse went, passing wards where children were sleeping, along corridors that smelt of disinfectant, up more stairs until Colm's legs were weary, and then at last into a small ward at the top of the building.

Colm was put into the bed near the window. It was cold and the pillow hard, and sometimes he raised his knees in a pyramid. Three electric lights were lit in the ward. The boys were all asleep and Colm noticed that they all wore the same shirts – white with black stripes. The young nurse came in, took his temperature, plugged his ear with wadding, and put out the lights.

Colm tried to sleep. He shut his eyes and began to count endless sheep as they came through a gap, but a jerk of pain in his ear brought his mind back to the hard pillow and the cold bed. Then he thought of the island: his mind wandered over familiar rocks, and rose and fell with the sea waves: the light of Kintyre carved the darkness: clouds commingled and departed in the sky; and evening with men on the roads and Paddy John Beg putting the mare in the field, building the stone-slap, cutting a twig from a bush and go off whistling past the edges of a lough, down to his house with the oil-lamp in the window and its beams falling into the open stable door ... His name on the rock would have spots of moss, but someday he'd go back and clean and scrape his name and bring Uncle Robert a new pipe. But if he were to die in the hospital ... He sat up in the bed and called to the boy beside him, but got no answer. Far away he heard the rattle of a dish, and getting out of bed he tiptoed down the ward and out on to the lighted corridor. He waited for a nurse to come, and when she came he asked for a drink of water. She scolded him and chased him back to bed.

In the morning three of the boys in the ward came over to Colm's bed and asked him his name, where he lived, and what ailed him. A nurse came round and while she was making the beds the boys sat on their pillows on the floor. She came over to Colm with a big bottle under her arm, and he heard a boy say that it was white mixture; she gave him some in a tumbler and he swallowed it in a gulp, made a wry face, and wiped his mouth with his shirt sleeve.

A boy gave out mugs and enamel plates stamped with blue letters B.U. – Belfast Union. The mugs were half-filled with tea and two pieces of bread were laid on the plates.

A nurse hung a white card on his bed, and a boy lent him a book and gave him half an apple. The first morning went slowly.

Outside it was raining. The seagulls were screaming and flying in flocks past the window. Trams were humming and somewhere a train whistled. Through the window he saw a seagull standing on one leg on the roof of a house and its companions flying around it. Colm wondered had it only one leg. A crow flew near it, turned its black head once, and dipped below the roof.

He sat up in the bed. Below him were the green lawns and the tarred paths, and against the boundary railings a row of trees with thinning leaves. The rain flung itself at the panes and a few spits of it fell on Colm's face; he loved the cold feel of it. On all the panes drops were forming, coming together, and wriggling like snail lines down to the sash. Outside, the rain slithered down the iron bars of the window and the ivy fluttered and shook the drops from its leaf-tips.

A nurse closed the window and the ward became stuffy and steamy. Soon a mist formed on the panes and when Colm could no longer see the rain he turned to talk to the boy beside him.

A nurse would come into the ward and have a look round, and sometimes when a boy was not in his bed he would hide until she went out. Once the young nurse came in and was talking to Colm when the matron entered. She came over to them, told the nurse to take the twists out of her stocking and to stop her dreaming. She looked at Colm's card and as she bent over him a little thread stuck out from the belt of her starched apron; Colm longed to pull it with his finger or bite it off with his teeth, but her cross face sent terror through him, and he lay stiff until she went out.

That night when the boys were all going to sleep, the sizzling started in his ear again. The boy beside him played with a piece of string, and Colm watched with regret the eyes closing and the twisted string lying on the blankets. He wanted to talk to him, to keep him awake for company, but he was afraid to break the imposed silence. A small light was lit above the frosted door. A hush hugged the ward.

The wind rustled in the ivy and people's hurrying feet echoed in the streets. The lamplight shone on the telephone wires and a light lit in a house opposite and went out. Then the moon rose up and he saw the shadows of the iron window-bars bending across the bed, and in the gaps of the moving clouds a skiffle of stars. Nearby a train whistled; it would be rushing now towards the station, the smoke unrolling from the funnel and glowing above the engine; and in the golden air of the carriage a boy would kneel on the seat and draw things with his finger on the window.

The train whistled again from afar and he knew he would hear it no more and that soon the noises would go from the city and there would be no company for him, but the cough from a sleeping boy or the shadow of a nurse passing the frosted door.

The following morning they got eggs for their breakfast. They were carried round in a bowl and the shell was peeled off them. The fellow that carried the bowl had a knife in his hand, he gave the big boys a whole egg and the small boys half an egg. He let Colm collect the mugs and the plates. That morning after the breakfast a nurse syringed his ear and it eased the pain.

In the forenoon they wheeled the beds to one side of the ward and started to play with a red rubber ball. The first time Colm kicked the ball his slipper came off and hit one of his companions on the head. Then someone kicked the ball too high and it hit an electric lamp and broke it in smithereens. They all fled to the bath-room and began to say: 'I never done it!' 'You done it!'

'No, I never!' said a fellow, combing his hair as if he never did anything.

'Come on and we'll get a brush and sweep it up,' said the eldest.

They all came out quietly, gathered up the glass chips, and threw them into the bin.

At dinner-time they had forgotten about the broken lamp. A man came round with bowls of soup on a tray. He had a coat, trousers, and waistcoat, made of corduroy, and when he stooped you could see the shine on them. His hair was brushed up in the front and he had a pair of grey slippers and no stockings. Colm heard some of the fellows calling him Sammy and others Willie, but the old man didn't seem to hear them as he handed out the bowls and mumbled to himself, 'This is the last soup yez'll get with my money. I'm going to leave this house and bring my pension book with

me. Yez'll not Sammy and Willie me then, for yez'd all die
of starvation!' But the next day he was back as usual, and
boys still shouted at him Sammy and Willie, and always he
chanted the same rhyme: 'This is the last soup . . .'

Visiting day arrived and the boys were in lively form,
sweeping the ward, and singing songs. A nurse brought in a
table and placed a black book on it. Some of the boys went to
the window to see if their mothers were coming, and began
talking excitedly when the visitors gathered outside the
ward-door. The nurse opened the door wide, and the
people trooped in, and soon the boys were sitting up in the
beds drinking lemonade and eating chocolate and buns.

Colm's mother came with a parcel hanging from her little
finger. She had sweets, oranges, and two books for him. She
sat on the chair beside the bed and gave him all the news:
how Alec had lost two pigeons in a race from Malahide,
and how Jamesy had got a job in McGrath's grocery,
weighing potatoes and going messages. Then she sat quite
still, not speaking, peeling an orange, and looking at him.
His hair had fallen in a fringe, his blue eyes were as bright as
beads, but his face was pale and his cheek bones lumpy.
Please God, he'd soon be out again, she said in her mind.
She looked at the white card hanging from the bedrail, but
could read no sense into the scraggy peaks and curves of the
graph.

When the bell rang she got up and pressed her hand
tightly on his forehead and went away.

Some of the smaller boys cried and their mothers came
back and gave them pennies. Then they all crowded to the
window and looked far down to the big door. The people
below looked up, waved their hands and smiled good-bye.

A nurse came round the beds and asked the boys had they
anything for the press. She wrote their names on the parcels,
but Colm had hidden his books under the mattress. They
played draughts, shared sweets, and exchanged books.

Colm got the loan of a cork gun and when the nurse went out he commenced shooting orange pips at the electric lamps. Then a flute band passed on the road and all the boys stopped their game to listen to the wet notes that came through the open window. Some of the boys began to sing the words to the tune:

> Do you think that I would let
> An ould Fenian get
> Destroy the loyal Orange lily-O ...

'Eh, boys, that's not fair!' said the biggest fellow in the ward. 'MacNeill's a Fenian, aren't ye?'

Colm nodded his head. 'Sing if you want to. I don't mind,' and he put his hand under the mattress for a book.

They all stopped singing and he heard them whispering amongst themselves at the bottom of the ward. The flute band had changed to another tune and only snips of sound could be heard as it turned into a side street.

That evening a minister came into the ward and gave a black hymn book to one of the boys, and the two of them began to sing a hymn about Heaven and the Angels. Everyone stared at them, but they paid no heed as they sang hymn after hymn, and in the pauses between the singing the minister said a few words to the boy. When he was going out he went round the beds and shook hands with all the boys, and when he came to Colm he gripped his hand tightly and playfully moved it up and down saying, 'Ah, let my hand go or you'll pull it off!' When he was going out the door he waved his hat to them and they all cheered.

And so the days went in brightened sometimes by the arrival of the minister or the talk of 'Sammy' or 'Willie' as he gave out the soup. In the mornings they awoke to the mug of tea and bread; then a line of boys would wait for the doctor outside the consulting room, boys with sore eyes, and some trembling with fear because they had to get their tonsils out. Colm would always wait to the last of the line, then go in, place his head on the nurse's lap, and off she would start to clean out his ear and all the time order him to keep steady.

Sometimes on a visiting day Alec would come and make jokes with all the boys in the ward; and once Jamesy arrived and told him about his job and the great football team that they had now. After that the days seemed to unwind themselves very slowly. From his bed he saw the trees outside losing their leaves and on windy days the leaves being swirled on to the wet roofs of houses or on to the pavements. He saw boys leaving and others coming; and then at last his day of freedom arrived – the doctor had examined him and told him that he was as right as the mail and ready to kick football anytime.

All that evening Colm whistled with delight and talked to the small boys who had just arrived and told them of the great sport that they would have later on; and at night he stood at the window and looked out on to the lighted streets. A motor car turned into the gate of the hospital, its lights shone on his face and turning round he saw his enormous shadow on the wall of the ward. Newsboys were shouting and he saw one jumping on to a lighted tram.

In the morning when he awoke the tea had been served and his mug lay on the floor at his bedside. A milky scum had formed on the top of it and because it was cold he drank it quickly.

In the afternoon a nurse brought him a red flannel coat and slippers and told him to sit at the fire until his mother arrived. Presently she came, carrying his clothes in a brown parcel. He felt very tall and thin when he was dressed. The coat was too small for him and his wrists stuck out of it. His mother made him shake hands with all the boys in the ward, and then out, down the stairs, through the big doors and into the cold open air and the wet lawns. At the top window all the boys were bunched, waving their hands through the bars. Colm waved to them, the porter opened the gate, and they passed out into the noise of the traffic and the trams.

Along Sandy Row they went. The streets were wet and the shadows of the chimneys on the slates. Steam arose from the horses' backs and here and there on the roads patches of oil shone with rainbow colours. Colm's head felt light. Everything was queer and people moved past him like creatures in a dream. At the top of the railway bridge a little man with an eye-shade on one eye and dusters in his pockets stood behind a tripod camera. As Colm and his mother approached he raised the palm of his hand: 'Steady, now, Missus, and I'll take your photo while-you-wait.' They walked past him as if he were a cardboard advertisement and then the mother said to Colm, 'Them's the quare frauds. They took Alec's photo not so long ago and after a couple of days you couldn't have seen the picture for the black fog that came on it.'

When he got into the kitchen a big blanket was hanging from the line making the place dark. Rover ran around barking and sniffing and licking his hands. The kitchen seemed very small.

'You're glad to be home, son,' said his mother, hanging up her coat behind the door. 'Rest yourself now on the sofa. I'll make you a drop of tea in a wee minute and send Clare for an egg.'

Clare stood in the middle of the floor smiling shyly at him. She had grown tall. On the wall he noticed two new pictures: one of P.H. Pearse and a group of men signing the Republican Declaration of 1916, and another of Thomas MacDonagh.

When Jamesy came home from work he brought Colm out to the yard to show him a tool-box that he had made and a shelf for pots and pans.

NINE

The first day that Colm went back to the College after his spell in the hospital the Dean had come round the classes, chewing a quill, and carrying in his hands a bundle of white envelopes. He came into Colm's class and gave each boy one of the envelopes.

'Now, boys, bring these home to your parents and get them to send the fees to me as soon as they can. You know, boys, it takes money to keep up the College and we are in debt already – terrible debt!' and he made curves with his hands to demonstrate its immensity, and kept sucking away at the quill which now and again rattled against his teeth. 'And we want money to build a new wing and to pay for the electric light that has just been installed. The House must be kept up to date, but it takes money. Now, like good boys, put these envelopes in a book in your bag and give them to your parents when you get home. Don't forget, for I'll come round again soon.'

Colm got an envelope like the rest of them, his mother's name written neatly across it. He put it carefully into his bag, but all through the day he kept thinking of Father Byrne and wondered had he stopped paying for him.

He didn't call into the library to exchange his book, but hurried home. It was Monday and when he arrived in the kitchen his mother was washing. A big bath sat between two chairs, and she had her sleeves rolled up and was busy rubbing the clothes up and down the wash-board. Her fingers were white and crinkled, and her wedding ring glittered.

The kitchen was congested with a warm soapy air, windows and pictures fogged, and the fire almost out. The red tiles were streaky with water and a steaming stack of twisted clothes lay at the corner of the table while others cooled in a bucket of cold water. With the noise of the scrubbing she didn't hear Colm as he came in. The bedraggled look of the kitchen overcame him with a sickening feeling, and he lay on the sofa, wearied by the walk from school, hungry because there was no sign of food, and sick at heart because of the letter in his bag. He'd show it to her in the evening, when all were out and no one in but their two selves.

As his mother straightened her back and threw a strand of hair away from her eyes she noticed him. 'Oh, you put the heart out of me! I didn't hear you coming in. Butter yourself a piece of bread and it'll stifle your hunger till I'm finished. I won't be long.'

He went into the scullery and cut a piece off the loaf. He buttered it, took a bite, and made a wry face. 'There's a soapy taste of the bread!' he shouted.

'No wonder; sure that's the ould knife I use for cutting the soap. Why don't you watch what you're doing!'

As he cut at the loaf again he could hear her above the chumping noise of the wash-board. 'Under God I don't know how you get so much dirt on your shirts. A body's back is nearly broke trying to get them white again.'

Then she held up a shirt and stuck a finger through a hole in it. 'Now how on earth did you get that!'

'That's Jamesy's shirt!' he replied.

'A body couldn't hold out to you fellows! I'm never done washing and darning and sewing. And I see the both of you have the boots kicked off your feet with that football!'

She bent again with great vigour, the water splashing over the bath, dripping down its sides and on to the floor. Once the soap slipped from the chair and slid across the tiles, coming to rest against the fender.

'Hand me that soap, Colm, please!' She was in bad form; he didn't know whether to go out or stay in. Her right sleeve fell down and she asked him to roll it up for her.

Then he sat on the sofa eating his piece of bread. Ink was on his fingers and spots of it on his face.

'Where did you get all the japs of ink?'

And he began to tell her about the school 'war' that they had during a free 'forty'. Suddenly she gave a shout and her arms came from the water, a needle sticking in one of her fingers.

Colm pulled out the needle, and a speck of blood came with it. She shook her hand in the air, sucked her finger and said, 'It's in agony!'

She sat on a chair and her face became very pale.

'Will I go out for Mrs Tully, Mother?'

'No, no, Colm, I'll be all right in a minute. It was the shock of it,' and she looked up at him and smiled faintly.

He went into the scullery to get her a drink of cold water, and as she sipped it he stood in the middle of the floor, looking helplessly at the bath with its bulging clothes, the shining bubbles on the wash-board, and the thin steam rising from the frizzling suds.

Later he turned the handle of the mangle, and handed up

the clothes when she stood on a chair in the yard to peg them to the line. He emptied the bath into the grate, and Clare came in from the entry and lifted the suds and ran about with them on her hands. He hung the bath on a nail on the wall and the washing was over.

Clare helped to wash the floor and black-lead the fender. Alec came in for his tea, shaved, and went out. Jamesy went to the pictures and soon the house stole a quietness from the evening.

Colm sat at the white-scrubbed table. His hands were washed, and under the gaslight with his white exercise opened in front of him he felt clean and refreshed. His mother moved about quietly for fear of disturbing him, taking down the brass candlesticks from the mantelpiece, blowing her breath on them and giving them a wipe with a duster. Then she sat on a chair, took the hairpins from her hair and began to comb it in front of her face. It was black and shiny and strong. She divided it neatly and began slowly to plait it, for her forefinger was still throbbing. 'I'm getting old, Colm; there is a few grey ones in it.'

From upstairs Clare shouted down for a drink. Then the house became very still and pure – the fireside shining, the tiles clean and cold, Colm bent over his books, and his mother in a white apron and her pink hands on her lap. She got up, put on her spectacles, and began to read the Litany of the Dead from her prayer book and peruse all her memoriam cards.

At the top of the black sofa Rover lay asleep. He whined, gave little grunts, and his legs twitched involuntarily.

'He's dreaming, Mother. I wonder what he'd be thinking of.'

'God knows! Maybe the Island.'

Colm sighed. 'I wonder what the house would be like now?'

'You wouldn't know it. It'd be all choked with nettles and

dockins. God be good to your poor father, but I often heard him say, "Nothing grows old as quickly as an empty house" – There's truth in that. But do your work now, Colm, it won't be long till your exams come round again.'

Colm bowed his head. He opened a book and took out the white envelope.

'Mother!' he said, but she didn't hear him, and he turned the pages of a Latin book and tried to translate a few more sentences.

'Mother!' he said again.

'What is it, son?'

He gave her the envelope and told her it was from the Dean in the College. She looked at her name and turned the envelope over.

'What's in it?' she asked.

'It's an account. The Dean gave them out to all the fellows today,' Colm replied, coming over beside her.

'If Father Byrne has stopped paying I don't know in under God what we'll do!'

She opened the envelope and pulled out a sheet of paper; written across it in ink were the words – *Father Byrne's pupil.*

'Oh, thank God!' she sighed, and let the letter fall on her lap.

'Why did they give me that at all?'

'I suppose now they didn't want to shame you in not giving you an envelope like the rest. Sit down now and write a long letter to Father Byrne and tell him how you are getting on.'

TEN

Colm tried to study hard and with Jamesy working late he looked forward to having the kitchen to himself in the evenings. But sometimes Mrs Heaney would come up and sit talking, her feet on the fender and a letter from Joe in her hands. His mother would take down Theresa's last letter from behind the clock on the mantelpiece and read it aloud, Mrs Heaney punctuating the reading with: 'Now, now! Fancy that! Och, och! Now, now!'

Jamesy had christened her Now-Now, and when Colm heard her saying these words he hid his face with a crooked elbow and sometimes burst out laughing and made an excuse that he was laughing at a joke in one of his books. But he felt uncomfortable when he heard them talking about Theresa.

'I hope it'll be a little girl she'll have,' Mrs Heaney was saying. 'I always like a girl to be at the head of a family. They're aisier to rear than boys. Boys are a heartbreak – a heartbreak! And no companionship with them! When they grow up they leave you and they're never in the house, always on the go!'

'Och, well now, Missus, I wouldn't say that. There's Colm there and you wouldn't know he's in the house – he's as quiet as a mouse. I must say they never gave me any trouble when they were babies except Jamesy, now and again, and it was his teeth that tortured him. But they were all good. Colm, I think, gave the least trouble.'

Colm hated to hear himself praised and he closed his books and took Rover for a walk. But when he came back again Mrs Heaney was still in the kitchen. She gave a glance at the clock as he came in, and then in a surprised tone she started, 'Now, now, I never knew it was so late. I must be goin' now, Mary; they'll be wonderin' what's keepin' me.'

'Wait till you get a wee drop of tea,' said Mrs MacNeill, pushing her gently down on the sofa. 'I won't be a minute. A wee drop in your hand. Sure, what hurry's on you the night?'

Mrs Heaney cast a glance of affectionate disapproval at Colm and nodded her head as much as to say, 'That's a terrible mother you've got.'

Then crouched over the fire with the cups on the hob, the chat still went on, and only at the arrival of Alec and Jamesy did she make her final bow.

'What does she want now?' Alec said as soon as the door closed on her heels. 'I never come in of an evening but that woman's clockin' round the fire! Has she nothing else to do but gossip morning, noon, and night!'

'Och, Alec, you're too hard on her,' answered his mother. 'She's a good holy woman.'

'God help us all!' said Alec derisively. 'Her over in the chapel, day in, day out, hammering her breast, groaning with piety, and the dishes stinkin' in the scullery. A holy woman! Show me her home first! If it's boggin' I wouldn't give that' – he snaps his fingers – 'for her soul. Half of them don't know what religion means! . . . What was she up about tonight?'

'She wanted to know if we had sent any shamrock to Theresa for St Patrick's Day.'

'It bates all how she can think of the excuses.'

His mother showed him a little harp made of green ribbon and yellow thread. 'She's a kindly soul, Alec. She bought that for Clare.'

'She may be kind, but you must admit that she's a damned nuisance when you see too much of her!' Turning to Jamesy: 'It's you and that 'Turf Man from Ardee' that brings her up. Can she not get a gramophone record of that song?'

The mother listened no more to his bantering and started to make the supper. Colm closed his books; he had still some work to do, but tomorrow was St Patrick's Day and there was no school. He sat on a chair and read the newspaper that Alec had brought in. The news was always the same: barracks attacked in Cork; rifles stolen; policemen shot; Sinn Féiners imprisoned; and curfew in Dublin.

'And what are they always fighting about?' Jamesy asked as Colm read out to them.

'To free Ireland; to make her a republic!' replied Alec. 'Ah, if the Orangemen here would love Ireland and fight for her we'd be a free country in no time. But they'll never do it – they live in the memory of King Billy, Prince of Orange, who delivered them from the Pope and Popery . . . What a bloody mix-up of a country!' and he laughed ironically over his cup of tea.

Sitting with the paper on his knees Colm saw the twisted life of the city: the fightings at football matches between Catholics and Protestants; the paintings on the gable-ends of King William on a white horse, his sword raised to the sky, and printed underneath: REMEMBER 1690 . . . NO POPE HERE. And in the Catholic quarters, the green-white-and-gold flag of Ireland painted on the walls with UP THE REPUBLIC. It was a strange city, he thought, to be living two lives, whereas on Rathlin Catholics and Protestants mixed and talked and danced together. It was all a terrible mix-up. He threw down the paper and went into the scullery. Shamrock floated in a bowl and he picked a spray of it for his cap because tomorrow was St Patrick's Day.

He got up early the next morning and went to an early Mass, so as to have a long day for himself and Rover. Alec was to go to a football final; he pinned green and white ribbons – the Celtic Football Club colours – to the side of his cap, put a wooden corncrake in one of his pockets, and took a pigeon with him so as to send home the half-time score to Jamesy.

Jamesy with his companions played football on the waste ground, glancing over to the house now and again to see if the pigeon had arrived. As soon as they saw it drop from the clouds and fly round and round the street they stopped playing and cheered. Presently it lit on the slates and they all ran over to the back of the houses. Jamesy, full of excitement, went into the yard, climbed the ladder quickly, and into the pigeon-shed. He rattled a dish of corn to coax in the pigeon, but it only walked to the edge of the spout and looked down into the yard. He shook the dish again, but the pigeon took fright, flew up behind a chimney, and sat with shoulders hunched and feathers ruffled. He waved a handkerchief at it, but it moved closer between two chimney pots till only its tail was visible.

'May the divil choke it!' he said, as he clodded a pebble at it. The pigeon didn't budge.

'Throw salt on its tail,' John Burns jeered.

'Sell it and buy a donkey,' from another.

'Don't bother yerself, Jamesy, sure we'll see the result in the paper,' said Croppy Caulfield. And they all went away from the back-door to continue their match along by the palings.

Jamesy tried again to entice it into the shed; he threw bread-crumbs up on the blue slates, but not a flutter came from the tail that peeped from between the chimney pots. In disgust he flung a handful of corn at it and joined his companions.

As he played he watched the roof. Suddenly a dog barked and the pigeon arose in the air, and then came swooping towards the shed, its wings stiffened in a V. It lit on the lighting-board, pushed the trapdoor with its head and hopped into the shed. At that moment the fellows roared with laughter for they had seen Alec passing into the back of the house.

Jamesy ran from the field. Alec was standing in the kitchen; his face was tired and worried.

'Who won?' Jamesy asked eagerly.

'Who won! ... There were riots and shootings and baton charges, and the match was unfinished ... I'm done with football matches in this town!' and he took the wooden corncrake from his pocket, broke it across his knee, and pitched it into the fire.

'Aw, sure you shouldn't take it to heart like that,' said the mother. 'Everything will be all right in a day or two. And they'll all be talking and laughing together again like old soldiers.'

'They'll never do it in this town! There's too much hatred, too much bitterness! I'm finished with it anyway for there's no pleasure in watching a football match where fellows carry guns in their hip-pockets!'

Ruefully Jamesy watched the corncrake crackling in the fire, and going outside met Colm and Rover as they came into the yard. Rover carried a stick in his mouth; his paws were soaking and his brown curly ears were dripping with water. He lay down with his forepaws resting on the stick and looked up at Colm with inviting eyes.

'You should have been with us, Jamesy. It was lovely up

on the mountain and Rover chased a rabbit.'

'When the summer comes we'll go up often and sail boats in the pit-dam,' said Jamesy. 'Hurry out now for we're going to pick a match.'

ELEVEN

Alec never went back to see a match though the football season was nearly over. He spent his Saturday afternoons with the pigeons, standing at the back of the house watching them fly over the street and over the mountain fields. Sometimes he entered them for a race, and at night he went down as usual to the bird-shops. He went alone now, for Jamesy was always working late on Saturday nights, wheeling large orders on a truck or pushing the heavy bicycle with the basket crammed with parcels on the handle bars.

On Saturday nights Colm stayed at home. Alec had bought him a magic lantern, and he used to hang a sheet on the door of the wee room and invite John Burns, Croppy Caulfield, and Sheriff McCann to see the films: clowns jumping through hoops; a boat race; making cocoa in a large factory; and a dark-green film that nobody could make out, but Colm always told his audience that it was a naval battle at sea. At school he exchanged films with Millar, who used to boast of his cinematograph that had a carbide generator.

One night the lantern went on fire, and while Colm was kicking the blazing tin into the yard Clare had run out to the street shouting and screaming, 'The house is on fire! The house is on fire!' Neighbours came running into the kitchen while Colm threw water round the lantern that hissed and fumed in the yard. His face was red, and in a nervous, hoarse voice he said: 'Oh, it's all right! It was only a wee bit of a blaze, that's all!'

When the neighbours went out again and the door closed on them he scolded Clare for raising such an hysterical alarm.

Later his mother came home and she had the whole story on her lips: 'What's that I hear about the house nearly being set on fire! . . . That's a nice performance. Well, I'm glad to see the end of that divil's toy for there was no peace while it was in the house!'

Colm had already collected the blue-burnt parts from the yard: the glass in the lens had vanished, and the spool and rod for the films were twisted and buckled beyond all worth.

Now that his own lantern was no more, he took to visiting Millar on a Saturday evening. He always went by the same way: down the Falls Road up Dover Street, across the Shankill Road, and, because it was May, saw the Orangemen cane-walloping big drums strapped to their shoulders, and a man with a flute to his mouth whistling away whenever the terrific noise of the drums had ceased. And then as he came into Millar's street with its high houses he could hear the drums rattling in the distance like shunting trains.

Timidly Colm approached the door and rapped gently. There was always a lovely smell of something roasting when the door was opened; and he was brought into the parlour where he stepped politely over the snips of patterns and thread on the floor, and sat in a corner beside the sewing-machine looking with a smile at the tailor's dummy with the tattered neck and the coats on hangers draping the door.

While Jimmy would be getting his cinematograph ready his mother would come into Colm with a glass of milk and biscuits, clasp her hands in front of her and say in a jovial way: 'The two of you will fail in your exams over the head of those old contraptions. It's out for a dander you should be in that lovely evening.'

Jimmy, standing behind her, would move his two false teeth up and down and wink cutely at Colm. Then the lantern would be placed on a box, water poured in the generator, and the burner lit; a knock would come to the door, and Jimmy and Colm would be chased up to the attic as someone had arrived to have a coat fitted or a frock made.

Up in the attic they would show the films over and over again, then Millar would get out his spring dumb-bells and put Colm through a number of arm-exercises that were supposed to make muscles like balls of steel. Then down the stairs again, tripping over the things in the dark, Jimmy plaguing his mother for a few pence, and then out into the street, stopping at the first shop to buy sweets, and later watching the practising Orange bands as they returned to headquarters for the night.

That June Colm and Jimmy sat for their examinations and both said that they had done poorly, but anyway they had the long holidays to enjoy before the official results would be published. Colm lay in bed in the mornings and laughed at Jamesy as he got up heavy-eyed for work. Later he washed the yard, and spent the whole day with Rover in the fields.

The night before the Twelfth of July the Orange bonfires were lighted and from the brickyard Colm, Jamesy, and their friends saw the sky reddening over the city and the chimneys in many streets glow fiercely in the leaping flames. Then in the still summer air the songs were carried to them: 'Dolly's Brae', 'Derry's Walls', 'The Sash My Father Wore', 'The Boyne Water', and 'God Save the King'.

'The Pope will get a quare scutching the night,' said a woman who had brought her child up to see the flames.

'It won't be long, Missus,' said John Burns, 'till the Fifteenth of August and we'll show them how to make a bonfire.'

They were filled with a wild frenzy of impatience as they saw the fires grow bigger. And as they were going home they were all making plans for their bonfire: Jamesy was to collect old boxes from his shop, Croppy Caulfield was to ask his da to get old bicycle tyres, and John Burns was to lead a gang of boys over McCrae's palings to chop down trees.

The next day Colm got up early and went down town to see the Orangemen marching. It was like a Sunday. Shops were closed and they had the whole town to themselves. They marched in four deep, most of them in navy-blue suits, hard hats, and orange sashes. Glossy-painted banners, some of biblical subjects, led each section, followed by a band. There were bands of all kinds: flute bands, brass bands, pipers' bands, accordion bands, all playing at once, with here and there men in their shirt-sleeves hammering the big drums. The air was alive with sound; the notes from the miscellany of instruments whirled in the air, interlaced, shrieked and descended to be sent sky-high again by the stone-crushing noise from the big drums. And all the time the men marched, strong and tough and gay. Small boys with sashes also marched, and once a man passed wheeled in his bath-chair, his sash round his neck, and the colour of death on his face.

'God love him!' said a woman near Colm, and gave him a special cheer for himself, and the man who was pushing the chair, straightened up, and there was strength of steel in his face.

That day passed in peace, but the fire of the leaders'

speeches smouldered for days in the minds of the common people, and towards the end of the month a mob of them, armed with sticks, invaded the shipyards and chased out the Catholic workers. Then riots began in the poorer parts of the city. Snipers hid on the roofs of houses and factories and swept the streets with bullets. The military were called out, and the lovely summer evenings were perforated by the rattle of rifles and machine guns.

At night the MacNeills prayed that the riots would cease, and thanked God that their street was quiet. But in the mornings they heard the newsboys shout: 'Twelve shot dead! Two hundred wounded.'

A paper was bought and Colm read out loud: how a brother was shot dead standing at a window in the Monastery and of the shootings in Ballymacarret and York Street. And the mother wrung her hands and said, 'God protect us all! Why can't they live in peace!'

For two weeks the shootings and the lootings continued. In the early evenings the streets were deserted and lorry loads of steel-helmeted soldiers passed to and fro. But in the middle of August peace came to the city again, and Jamesy and the boys from the street went around collecting boxes for their bonfire. If the Orangemen celebrated the Twelfth of July, the Catholics celebrated the Feast of the Assumption, and the Ancient Order of Hibernians carved out A.O.H. on trees and byre doors, marched with green sashes, drank porter, talked about Home Rule for Ireland while the Sinn Féiners fought and died for a Republic. In Jamesy's street half of the people were Hibernians and half Sinn Féiners, but on a night like the Fifteenth of August they all joined together and contributed to the bonfire.

All through the day boxes, trunks of trees, old baskets from the bakery were being heaped in a pile in the middle of the street. Mrs Tully gave an old ruptured sofa with the straw gorging out at the bottom and Joe McAteer parted with the planks that he had nailed to the shed the previous year.

As darkness set in, the street was crowded. Women with arms folded stood at the open doors, the children crying around them, 'Ma, let me stay up to see the bonfire!'

Jamesy and Colm put tyres round a little boy till they covered his head, then they swirled the tyres one by one on top of the pile, and laughed when one caught in the branches of a tree and hung dangling.

The paraffin was shaken over the pyramid of fuel and cheer upon cheer arose when the first flames stretched into the air. All gathered round ready to sing, and an old woman with a crakey voice shouted, 'Sing up there!' Immediately the boys and girls burst out:

> Soldiers are we, whose lives are pledged to Ireland;
> Some have come from a land beyond the wave,
> Sworn to be free, no more our ancient sireland
> Shall shelter the despot or the slave . . .

And when they had finished they shouted 'Up the Rebels! Up the Republic!'

Boys came round with bin-lids and circled the fire like wild Indians, rattling, shouting, and yelling. Showers of sparks sprayed in all directions, and leaping flames lit up the red brick houses, and crackled the black twigs whose leaves shrivelled in the great heat. White bubbles of moisture hissed on the ends of the branches that lay at the edge of the fire. Some children who were put to bed stood in their shirts at the top windows looking down. A gush of sparks came from a squib and girls screamed when it went off with a bang.

'Look at the rocket!' shouted Jamesy, and all eyes searched the sky to see a curving rocket trail behind it a tail of golden sparks.

At midnight the fire was at its best and boys climbed up

the lamp-posts and put out the lights.

Paint on the windows began to blister and little girls burst them with their fingers. Then Mrs Tully came out with jugs of water, threw them over the window-sashes, and steam arose slowly and vanished. Colonel Magee's pom was lying at the door and someone flung a squib at it, and it ran yelping up the street into the darkness.

'On with that one!' shouted Jamesy, as he helped a boy to throw a large box on the blaze.

Then suddenly all the commotion stopped; policemen came up the street and chased the crowd for singing rebel songs.

'It's a bloody shame!' said a woman from the shelter of her doorway. 'Sure they're doin' no harm. It's well seen yiv little else to do!'

'They wouldn't chase the Prods when they had their bonfire on the Twelfth of July,' said another.

The police took no notice as the women jeered at them when they were going out of the street again. One by one the crowd stole back to the bonfire and Alec produced his melodeon and played Irish dances, many doing reels at the edge of the flames. All through the night they sang and danced, and only when the stars were fading from the sky did they leave the warmth of the fire for bed.

In the morning a circle of white and black ash lay in the street, some logs were still smouldering, and children were gathering up the red-burnt nails that were strewn around the edges.

TWELVE

The end of the bonfire marked the end of the summer holidays. In a week's time Colm was back at the College; Clare went into her new class and already, in the evenings, was reading her new books with the help of her mother; Jamesy was still employed as message boy, and Alec had joined the Irish Republican Army. He sold the pigeons, for he had no time for them and no heart to work with them.

Colm took possession of the shed, scraped it out, swept the floor, and under the narrow glass window he got Jamesy to help him to make a shelf for his books.

For the first week after he went back to school he climbed every evening up the ladder to the shed. His mother had given him a stool; Jamesy had made a table for him out of old butter boxes; and so he was able to do his exercises and learn his lessons. Finished, he would stand for a while at the window which overlooked the yard-walls. From there he could see the men digging the brown clay in the pit, the glint of a shovel as it caught the sunlight, and the long line of bogies filled with clay moving slowly towards the sheds. Beyond was the white mountain lonin, and looking at it he often thought of the rocky pool at its end, the cold water forever gushing and tumbling into it, and the little drinking tin sitting on a flat stone. He knew every hollow on that mountain, saw them being filled with sun-shadow, and the whole mountain grow black and close at approaching rain. He would stand and think of Knocklayde and compare it with the mountain before him: the one barren and desolate, the other green and near. Then he would turn away, do some dumb-bell exercises, pencil his height on the boards of the shed, and then out to the waste ground to play football until dark.

Sometimes when he would be leaving the shed for the evening he would see one of Alec's pigeons had returned and was looking for the entrance. He would then have to take the boards off the trap-door, spread newspapers over his books and let the pigeon in. In the morning Jamesy would tear two holes in a paper bag, put the pigeon inside, and take it back to its owner.

But Colm's seclusion didn't last long. Riots broke out again, and he left the quiet of the pigeon-shed for the noise and companionship of the kitchen, once again to listen to Mrs Heaney talking now about Theresa's newborn baby girl, showing his mother woollen coats that she had knitted for it, and all the time Clare pestering him with her sums. Tired of the chatter he would stand at the door and listen with a growing fear to the shots in another part of the city or a man just up from the town telling him about the number that were shot dead in Ballymacarret, and that curfew was being declared over the whole city.

'It must be near the end of the world,' said Mrs Heaney when she heard about the curfew and everyone to be in the house at half-past ten at night.

The first night of the curfew the MacNeills had gathered into the house early and Mrs Heaney had not come up for her usual chat. Alec slept in her house, for raids were now frequent and IRA suspects were being arrested and interned. Jamesy was making a scooter for the boy next door, Clare was in bed, and the mother was darning socks. They argued over the lighting of the gas, wondering if it were allowed to be lit during curfew. Jamesy went upstairs and looked out of the back-room window to see if the rest of the neighbours had their gas lit.

'Light up!' he shouted as he came running downstairs again.

'Quit the shouting,' Colm said to him when he came into the kitchen.

'Surely to goodness we can talk during curfew,' replied Jamesy cockily.

'S-s-s-h,' put in the mother, and they all hushed at once.

The armoured car rattled up the street and throbbed in the kitchen. Their eyes were alert and steady with fear as it passed the house; and then with suppressed delight they heard its noise fade in the distance. A lightness came over Colm, he gulped the air noisily, and felt a hollowness within him. Jamesy bent to the scooter again, and once when he hammered the wheel loudly Colm said irritably, 'Sure you can do that in the morning!'

'I'll do it now that I'm free and no other time,' and he gave the axle another whack with the hammer.

'Stop it, I tell you!' Colm shouted as Jamesy took a few nails from a box.

'Tell him to stop the hammering, Mother. You wouldn't know whether they were listening at the door and they'd think it was guns were were making.'

'And how could a child's scooter be guns?' Jamesy looked up at him, his face red from stooping.

'Put it away, I tell you, or I'll smash it in bits!'

'Try it on till ye see what you'll get.'

'Och, och,' intervened the mother, leaving down darning. 'Never since God made me did I see boys who fought so much. God knows there's enough fighting outside than you to be bringing it inside. Put everything away for the night and we'll say the rosary.'

They offered the prayers up for peace, for Alec's protection, and implored Our Blessed Lady to safeguard the house. Once Rover barked when they were at their prayers and Colm turned out the light and patted the dog's head. Then they knelt in silence, waiting any moment for the back-door to be battered or shots fired into the kitchen. But nothing happened, the dog went to sleep again, and the mother continued the prayers. When the rosary was ended Colm went off to bed.

He stood at the window of his room looking at the waste ground and the bits of broken delft catching the moonlight. Above the dark palings the trees were black and through the branches he saw thin clouds riding up the sky. It was very still, and he thought of the same moon glittering on the sea in Rathlin, filling the valleys with shadow, shining on the walls of his old home, and wetting the rock-face of his den with cold light. Inside the deserted house there would be the bare hearth, yellow straw in a corner, and a snail weaving its silver line across a mouldy sack . . . He felt weary and sick. He knelt on the bare boards and covered his face with his hands. He leaned forward on the bed-clothes, felt his warm breath flung back upon his cheeks and the dusty smell from the blankets. His mind wavered and fell into a dream, and it was Jamesy coming up to bed that wakened him.

'You're praying a lot tonight, Colm,' he remarked jovially. 'Are you doing a Novena?'

Colm did not answer. In silence and in the light of the moon they undressed, but, once in bed, Colm regretted his sullenness and felt the words form in his throat, the words that he had said to his brother for a long time – 'Good night, Jamesy.'

'Good night, Colm.'

THIRTEEN

A week afterwards the house was raided. It was Saturday. Alec had gone out after nine o'clock to Mrs Heaney's, and the rest had gone to bed before curfew. Then after midnight there came a loud knock at the front door. Colm jumped out of bed and went into his mother's room; the light from the street lamp shone through the curtained window, and he could see her gripping a coat in front of her. Clare was still asleep.

'What will we do, Mother?' he asked in a rising whisper.

'Wait till they knock again.'

He went to the window and peeped out. He saw the soldiers, their bayonets and helmets shining in the lamp light.

They knocked again. 'Open! Military!' a man ordered.

Jamesy came into the room, his teeth chattering.

'Get you two back to your bed and I'll open the door,' said the mother, going out on to the landing.

Colm and Jamesy sat up in the bed. They felt cold and

couldn't keep their limbs from trembling. The door opened and they heard the clink of steel in the hall. Then a light made the shadow of the bannisters jig across the bedroom door. A military officer came into the room, an automatic pistol in one hand and an electric torch in the other. He lit the gas jet and looked at the two boys in bed.

'What is your age?' he asked Colm.

'Fifteen past,' Colm answered in a quaky voice.

'And yours?'

'Fourteen and a half,' replied Jamesy.

'You have an elder brother, haven't you? . . . Where is he?'

'He went down to the country for the week-end,' lied Jamesy, his courage gaining strength from the polite tones of the officer.

The officer turned to the chest of drawers, and a little soldier with his rifle and bayonet by his side looked over the rail of the bed and winked at Colm and Jamesy. They nervously smiled back at him. The officer gripped the two knobs of the top drawer and they came off in his hands.

'It always does that,' said Jamesy, and he hopped out of bed in his shirt, put his forefingers in the holes where the knobs had been, and pulled out the drawer.

The officer lifted up a few of the contents: old jerseys, patches for shirts, three yellow gritty candles tied with a scapular, and a few faded newspapers.

Outside on the landing a policeman was talking to the mother. He placed his hand gently on her shoulder, 'Now, like a good sensible woman, give me the gun now and there won't be a word about it.'

'What gun?' she raised her voice – 'There's no gun here!'

'S-s-s-h,' said the policeman, glancing into the room at the military officer as if it were a confidence trick between the woman and himself. He patted her on the shoulder and whispered:

'Give it to me now and it will be all right. There'll not be a word about it, not a word about it, I tell you.'

She shrugged her shoulders. The military officer came out and into the other room. He flashed his light round, and when he saw Clare asleep in the bed he turned down the stairs, and the policeman followed. As they were going out to the street the policeman turned back; they heard him search around the scullery and the kitchen. Then there was a noise of breaking glass; Rover started to bark and the policeman hurried from the house.

The lorry rattled down the street and soon everything was quiet except Rover who was sniffing loudly at the front door.

The mother turned out the gas and in the dark sat on the edge of the boys' bed.

They remained for a while in silence and then they heard Rover's sharp claws on the oil-cloth of the stairs. He came into the room and walked round and round in the dark. No one spoke and he jumped on to the bed and licked the boys' faces.

The mother patted the dog and said: 'It's well Alec wasn't in or he'd have a hard bed tonight.'

'S-s-s-h!' replied Colm. 'I believe there's somebody downstairs.'

'Rover would have barked! Wait and I'll look.' The mother lit a candle and went down. Rover followed her.

In the kitchen her bare feet tramped on a piece of glass. She lit the gas and there on the wall were Alec's two pictures, *Thomas McDonagh* and *The Signing of the Republican Declaration*, smashed and torn. She called to Colm and Jamesy.

'It was the peeler did it! The time we heard him walking in the kitchen!' affirmed Jamesy.

They went back to bed, but were too excited to sleep, and in the morning they all arose earlier than usual. Alec came in for his breakfast and they all began telling him about the raid:

Jamesy about the wee soldier that winked at them over the rail of the bed; Colm about Rover walking round and round like a dog in a fever; and the mother about the policeman plaguing her for a gun.

'What was he like? What way did he talk?' asked Alec.

'He talked, now, I'd think, like a south-of-Ireland man. He had a brogue anyway and a sweet tongue it was too.'

'Be God, but there's something rotten about the Southern character when they can breed so many peelers of that type! A nice not-a-word-about-it he'd have said if he'd been lucky enough to get a gun!' And as he took his breakfast he told them about fellows that were arrested last night. 'When I was coming up the street,' he said, 'I met the postman and he was telling me that six were arrested in the Kashmir Road.'

He had the same story to tell every morning, and when Colm was going to school he would see lorry loads of prisoners, brought in from the country, and singing rebel songs as they were conveyed to Crumlin Road Jail. People would shake their fists at them and sometimes groups of women at street corners would jeer and wave Union Jacks. Colm would rejoice secretly when he would hear the Crumlin Road echoing with the 'Soldiers' Song'. Now and again he would stand too long and be late for school; he would try to sneak up behind the trees of the College avenue, and when he had entered the vestibule and thought all was safe, there would be a rustle of a soutane and the President would be before him: 'What's the meaning of this, Colm? Late again!' he would say in his sing-song voice; and if he were in good form he would let him off. 'Maybe you had to feed the baby; tut-tut, too bad, now! . . . Run on to your class like a good boy and don't let it occur again.'

Colm would trot away from him, down the corridor, and into his Mathematics class. They had a new master and he was easy. He was small, wore black clothes, and a claw-hammer collar which left room for his large Adam's apple to move up and down. His face was pale; his forehead was narrow and black hair stood up from it as thick as a clipped hedge. He always cut himself shaving and every morning he had pieces of white paper stuck here and there on his neck and chin. They nick-named him 'Birdy' for his voice was tight and squeaky and when he put his hands under his coat he looked like a narrow little penguin.

He always prefaced his teaching by a few remarks on 'Obedience' and 'How to become a Gentleman'. But as time went on and no cane was produced the boys came in frequently without having done their home-work and he said nothing to them. Then they got knitting needles, darning needles, and tuning-forks, and hammered them into secret crevices in the desks, pinging them with their fingers or toe-caps whenever Birdy turned to the blackboard. Tins with pebbles inside them were hidden in the presses alongside the wall, cords were attached, and at intervals the strings would be pulled and tins would rattle in every part of the room. Sometimes when Birdy went to investigate, the class hissed, stamped and pinged the needles; and he would look at them with scorn and say in a rancorous voice. 'You Belfast unmannerly tykes!'

But his preaching to them was of no use. They boldly vied with each other in lettering the quadrilaterals on the black-board B-I-R-D, and when the class laughed the teacher would look at them with astonishment. Sometimes when the lesson was over and the master gone out Millar would stand up and say: 'Aw, look here, chaps, it isn't fair – Birdy's a decent spud. You wouldn't play on Cogs, I bet you. No fears! He'd slaughter us all!'

'Look who's talking,' they'd chorus. 'Throw Millar out, boys. Pitch him out! He's a traitor!' Someone would hit him on the head with a book, and when the next master would step into the room he would be looking at the class through a haze of dust.

But one day towards the end of the term when Christmas was drawing near and rifle shots cracked just outside the windows the fellows were restless. Birdy brought in *Ballygullion*, a book with humorous stories, to read to them and to keep them quiet, but at the first joke the class roared loudly and prolonged it so much that he shut the book in disgust and turned to do geometry. 'Aw, sir,' they all said, 'read the funny book and we won't laugh.'

He paid no heed to their plaintive cries and they became rowdier. He raced angrily at a few boys to give them the cane, but they would not hold out their hands, and the rest of the class pinged the needles and rattled the tins. He made a speech, appealing to their Catholicity, to play up and play the game; but when he was going out they stamped their feet and cheered, and the President dashed into the room.

His face was stern and pale, a stout cane by his side. A great fear swept over the class. The door of the room lay wide open and the cloud of dust that had risen from the floor was now settling softly on the boys' heads and on the surfaces of the desks. The teacher had gone out. The President looked around the class, his cane nervously slapping his soutane. He pressed the finger tips of one hand on Colm's desk and Colm saw the clean finger nails whiten.

'Stand out – the boys who made that noise!'

No one spoke; no one moved; nothing stirred except the softly falling dust. Colm tried to compose himself, but his heart pounded loudly and the blood burned his cheeks. His mind ran backwards and forwards like a shuttle; it would mean expulsion; it would be terrible to be sent home. He saw Uncle Robert propped in the bed and urging him to tell the truth no matter what happened. He rubbed his hands up and down the sides of his corduroy trousers.

The President's voice came again, more sternly, shivering

over the class like the echo of a rifle. 'I give you one more chance. Stand out – the boys who had any part in that noise.'

Colm found himself rising to his feet and moving out on to the floor. The priest looked at him. A blurred picture of Father Byrne fogged in his mind and he regretted having stood out. Other boys were coming out now: Jimmy Millar, Chit McCloskey, and Big Edwards. Edwards put his glasses in his pocket and his naked-looking eyes blinked like a person coming out of a dark room. Millar was rubbing his hands. Colm's head was lowered and when he raised it he saw the pale faces of the boys in the desks and their eyes large with fear, and the President's thumbs white with chalk and a button hanging loose on his soutane.

The President looked silently at the class and then turned to the four boys on the floor. He stretched out his hand oratorically and said in a muscular voice: 'Are these the four only manly men in this class? Four boys could never had made all that noise! Is there no Truth left in this house? No sense of honour or decency? Is that what you learn from your priests on Sunday – to practice deceit and lying? Is it? Listen to those shots outside! Is it any wonder that this city is the way it is – purged and racked and scourged? And you to be the citizens of tomorrow . . . I am not going to punish you,' – addressing the four on the floor – 'but I am going to punish all these other lying, good-for-nothing fellows!'

When he had done caning he said: 'And what's more, until further notice stay in here at lunch-hour, but you four can have your play as usual.' And with that he left the room.

Edwards stood up and over the heads of the crying boys he began in a mincing voice: 'Now, my dear boys, I always knew what would come of your rowdyism. I always told you, James Harte and Michael McFreely and Mulhern, that your conduct has been outrage-e-e-ous, stamping about the room like night-tripping fairies in army boots.' They all gave tremulous little laughs for he had mentioned the three quietest boys in the class.

Millar was about to make a speech when 'Cogs' entered, a tall man with a short red moustache and loose tweed clothes. He walked on his heels with his knees slightly bent. Everyone was afraid of him.

In the cold mornings he always stood against the gas stove, scratching his legs and again as they became too hot. He would shut his eyes and say: 'Now I'll call boys out at random. Come out to the board the second boy in from the last desk at this side.' With eyes shut, his cane outstretched in the direction of the desk, he would drawl out the words. And so it went on: boys being called out to the board to write down tenses of different French verbs, missing them, and Cogs dashing across from the stove to give them three flippers on each hand. After the first slaps the boys would squirm and moan with pain, hoping Cogs would have compassion on them and let them off with two. But he was acquainted with all their dodges and he would stand beside them, tapping them on the bowed shoulders: 'Come on, don't be wasting my time. If you were afraid of these slaps you'd learn your verbs at home. We must get three exhibitions out of this class in French.'

Many a slap Colm got from Cogs, coming back to his desk, placing his bruised hands under his warm oxters, and then between his thighs, his feet jigging with the pain. Cogs would shout: 'Look up here, boy. How will you know your verbs if you don't pay attention?' And Colm would look up and see, through the film of tears, blurred images of boys and Cogs himself diminished and far away, standing at the stove.

Then one day as he was warming himself as usual against the stove the plaster from the ceiling fell and broke in a thousand pieces upon his head. Millar laughed and Cogs, flakes of plaster on his moustache and his clothes as white as that of a flour-man, came down to Millar and trounced him with the cane for having the audacity to laugh at his misfortune. He had to leave the class and go to the kitchen to be cleaned and brushed, and while he was away Edwards looked up at the ragged hole in the ceiling and said: 'I wish, lads, it had been the bloody roof that had fallen on him.'

FOURTEEN

When the good weather came the stove was no longer lighted, but Cogs had left the College and had gone to teach in England. New masters came regularly, but the city with its riots was too wild for them, and they only stayed for a few weeks and departed for quieter places. But amongst the old masters and the boys there was great comradeship: little home-work was given to the pupils, and the masters took any excuse if it were not done. Even Father Alby became soft and he used to smack his hands and say: 'When the hurly-burly's done, then we'll have the fun!'

Colm loved the school, but hated the coming of night with its curfew, the desolate streets, the volleys of shots ringing out and his mother saying: 'That shooting is very near; it might be the Kashmir Road,' or, 'They're gettin' it in Marrowbone the night! God look down on them!'

And when he went to bed he tried to sleep by thinking of the island; but, in the morning, he awakened not to the cry of gulls or the sound of the sea, but to the rattle of early trams and milk-carts and the newsboys shouting the latest ambush from Cork or a shooting in another part of his own city. Then down to his breakfast of crisp, fried bread, listening to Alec as he read the paper: 'In the South they have to fight one war and that's a political one. Here we have to fight a religious and a political one. Good God, I wish they could all love Ireland and love each other in this city.'

Colm would stop eating as he listened to him, and his mother would touch his elbow: 'Eat up, Colm, it's long till three o'clock.' A knock would come to the door and she would lift the jug and come in again: 'The milkman was telling me that there were ten shot dead in York Street!' Colm's stomach would become tight and sickish, and he would rise from the table, leaving his breakfast half-finished.

'Och, Colm, you're eating nothing these times. Are you not feeling well?'

'I'm not hungry, Mother,' he would answer with a nod of his head.

And then when he would be ready for school: 'Did you say your prayers this morning? ... Watch yourself, Colm, and hurry home. Won't you?'

He would hurry out with his bag of books, down the Falls Road, looking up at the houses for fresh bullet-marks. Policemen would be in groups and an armoured car at a corner that separated Catholic streets from Protestant streets. Everything would be alert and fearful. Here and there a handcart with its legs in the air would be in the middle of a street; cobble-stones dug up in heaps or holes made so that the armoured cars and police 'cages' could not get past.

Then one morning he was very late and Alec gave him the money for the tram. The tram-conductor was very excited and at every stop he shouted. 'We mightn't get down the road at all. There's sniping going on, all the morning.'

Some people turned home again at his warning and the half-empty tram passed down the Falls Road. Nearing Conway Street shots ran out, and Colm and the other passengers lay flat on the corrugated floor. There was a crack like a stone through ice and when the tram stopped in the shelter of a mill a man stood up beside Colm with blood claw-streaming from a wound in his hand. 'I'm hit!' he said.

Colm ran down the stairs of the tram and on to the road. He turned to go home. The road was deserted and the sun shining. 'Cage' cars were racing up and down, the rifles peeping out. The tram had gone on its way at terrific speed.

Colm ran down a side-street. All the doors were closed. He saw a man in his shirt-sleeves firing a revolver towards the Protestant quarters. A dog was running up and down barking. Colm knocked at a door, but shots rang out close to him and he ran off, going from one side of the street to the other. At last he saw a door slightly open and he pushed it quickly and closed it behind him. He was standing in a sour-smelling kitchen, coke burning on the fire, and crusts of bread on the floor. A woman was sitting with a crying baby on her lap.

'Good God!' she said. 'I thought you were Harry. My man went out ten minutes ago for sweet milk and he's never back yet ... Sure you shouldn't be out to school a morning like that! What was yer Ma thinkin' about?' Before Colm could reply somebody kicked the door impatiently and the woman ran with the child under her arm.

A man stumbled into the kitchen with an empty jug in his hand: 'What'd ye close the bloody door for? D'ye want me bloody well riddled?' he shouted; and then seeing Colm he lowered his voice. 'There's not a taste of milk to be had for love nor money. There hasn't been a milkman seen this morning.'

'What'll we give the child, Harry?'

'Boil him some water and sugar.'

'He'd no more look at it than he would at castor oil!'

'Try and get him to sleep. They'll hardly keep shootin' the whole bloody day.'

He turned to Colm; his black hair uncombed, his face unshaven, and a brass stud in his shirt. 'This is a damned town-and-a-half to be livin' in. No work in it and them that have work can't get down till it.'

'There was a man shot in the tram I was in,' said Colm.

'There was a woman shot stone dead on the other side of the street. There's a sniper on the mill all the mornin' and you daren't put your nose out the door.'

Shots cracked fiercely and the man instinctively ducked his head.

'Jesus, Mary, and Joseph!' said the woman, blessing herself. 'That's near!'

'Them's our fellas returnin' the fire,' the man replied.

A ricocheting bullet pinged away over the slates, and Colm edged from the window and sat on the bare stairs. The woman noticed the colour leaving his face and she handed the child to her husband and brought Colm a drink of cold water.

'Don't be frightened!' said the man. 'That's nothin' when yer used to it.'

Everything became very still. The sun shone in the window, and they could hear no trams running except the ambulance whizzing up the road and its whistle blowing. 'There's another poor divil hit!'

The woman put the child in the cradle, gave it a dummy tit, and began to rock with her hand.

Then from upstairs came the shouts of more children: 'I wan' up, Ma.'

'Lie down there!' she shouted up to them. 'I'll go up with the taws in a minute. Yer not gettin' up this day and the whole street gettin' killed and murdered!'

But they continued to cry and the man stamped up the boarded stairs. Colm could hear him in the back-room of the house: 'Lie down now and keep away from the windows!'

And all the time the woman rocked the cradle, her back to the door of the wee room. From within came a thump-thump on the wall.

The woman got to her feet. 'Here, son, watch the child till I see what the ould wan wants.'

As Colm rocked the cradle he could hear the woman shouting in the wee room, 'No, he's not away yet. The shoemaker's puttin' heels on his boots; he can't go out till he gets them . . . Ai, they're away to school an hour ago.'

He could hear the coughs from an old woman.

A shadow passed the window and he saw an armoured car. He shut his eyes and crouched low as he heard the dic-a-dic-a-dic-a-dic-a from the Hotchkiss gun.

'Good God, that's wicked!' said the woman as she came from the room. 'It's well, son, yer in out o' that!' She took her prayer beads from a nail in the wall. The shooting stopped. The children upstairs were crying and the man was trying to comfort them.

'It's sometimes a good thing to be stone deaf,' the woman was saying. 'There's my poor mother in there and she doesn't hear a thing nor know a word of what's going on . . . God's good to her these days in takin' her ears from her.'

She took the crying child from the cradle and brought it into the wee room. Outside in the street everything was still, and in the sunbeam at the window three flies were zig-zagging.

The man leaned over the bannisters. 'Are you there, Annie? I think it's over for the day. Make a drop of tay for I'm starvin'.'

'I'll make it, but ye'll have to have it black!'

When they were taking the milkless tea they saw through

the window a baker's cart ambling down the street, and heard doors opening and people talking.

'It's over for a while anyway,' said the man, and he got up from the table to open the door for Colm.

Women with black shawls over their heads were making out now to the shops, and in open doorways many were gossiping. At the head of the street a policeman stopped Colm and searched his schoolbag, and once on the Falls Road again he hurried home. Trams were running now; shops were opening, and milkmen moving down the side-streets.

That night the names of the dead and wounded filled two columns of the paper. Jamesy was reading them: 'DEAD: SAMUEL WILTON – he'll be a Prod; MICHAEL KELLY – he''ll be a Catholic.'

'Jamesy!' shouted the mother, giving him a clout on the side of the head. 'Is that the way you were reared! To be talking like that about the dead! God have mercy on them all!' and she took the paper from him and sent him up to his bed.

A few weeks afterwards the College was raided. Colm arrived one morning to find soldiers with fixed bayonets lined outside the gates of the avenue. It was nine o'clock and many of the day-boys had gathered in groups and were wondering if they should go home again. Those who had bicycles went off and the rest stayed.

After about two hours soldiers and police came marching down the avenue, jumped into the lorries, and when they moved off, Colm and the other boys cheered loudly and raced through the gates.

In the corridor he met Millar and Chit McCloskey. Everyone was talking and shouting and the boarders were running wild.

'Aw, Colm,' said Millar, 'you missed the sport. It was great gas. We were all put into the study hall while the soldiers searched. Father Black sat in the rostrum and he paid as much heed to the raiders as he would to the window cleaners. But wait to you hear this. They found a dead crow up the chimney. And at Piper Nolan's desk there was a loose board and a soldier put his bayonet under the board and lifted it up. Piper's face went as red as a beetroot. Do you know what he found?'

'How the dickens would I know?' answered Colm impatiently.

'They found rusty roots of apple, hard black banana skins, crusts of bread, mouldy cheese, caramel papers galore, empty packets of Woodbine, and "Buffalo Bills"!'

'Oh, boys!' said McCloskey. 'You should have seen the face of Piper!'

Father Black saw it all after the soldiers went away and he said that there was as much rubbish there as would raise a plague.

'If the President gets to hear about it,' put in Chit, 'and all the empty fag packets, I wouldn't like to be Piper!'

Big Edwards came over to them where they leaned against the corridor wall.

'Do you know what I heard, lads?' he said.

'No, tell us,' replied Millar. 'I am sure nobody else has heard it.'

'They searched Father Black's room because he wouldn't notice them in the Study Hall and they confiscated an old air gun that he had for pelting cats off the wall.'

Millar laughed, but Edwards continued: 'If you don't believe me, ask Father Black himself. Do you know what else they did? They broke his golf sticks thinking that they would be drilled and filled with bullets.'

'Come on, boys,' said Chit, 'we have enough of Edward's raid.'

They ran out of the corridor on to the football field. No bell rang until two o'clock and then they didn't mind for they had Father Daly for English. He gave them an essay to write on 'The Raid'. When they had finished he read Colm's aloud to the class: 'Most realistic picture ... There's a boy who can use his eyes and his ears!'

Millar, seated on the other side of the room, tried to attract Colm's attention, but Colm had his head lowered; his face was blazing as he heard the praise, and in his heart he hoped that Father Daly would never find out the truth.

FIFTEEN

Coming home from school Colm saw, day after day, youths painting on the gables: NO PARTITION — WE WANT OUR COUNTRY. There were to be elections soon, but Colm took no interest in them except to hear Alec talking at tea-time: 'If Ireland is partitioned now it will take a long time before she's made one again. And when unity does come I heard a man say that it would take a hundred years before these people here'd fit into a National life. They hate the real Ireland! And 'tis a pity for they're hard workers and good fighters.'

After the tea Colm would go up to the pigeon-shed to do his home-work. He would stand as usual at the little window looking at the mountain, seeing long scaffolding of rain falling in front of it, dropping like smoke over the fields, and men racing for shelter to the brickyard. He would hear the shouts of women calling in their children and the children giving joyful screams as they raced home. A woman would pluck the clothes off the line at the approach of the shower; hens with trailing wings would race madly from the waste ground; a goat would run round and round on its tether, me-e-e-e-eh loudly, and then stand hunched with its back to the mountain and the oncoming rain.

Soon the rain would reach the street, pelt harshly on the slates, and swish against the pigeon-shed. As Colm listened to it his mind would race to his Uncle Robert, remembering how he used to draw great delight and comfort from the lonely sound of rain. Quickly the shower would pass, leaving the clay in the brickyard pit a dark brown; the goat would shake its ears and the blue-shining slates reflect the chimneys.

Colm would get to his work before the dusk would sweep the light from the shed.

But soon the warm May evenings arrived with their long hours of sunlight; and he would now see the hens lying in scratched-out holes, people sitting on newspapers on the grassy banks, Mrs Tully putting her flower pot in the sun, a woman throwing out a condensed milk tin and Rover running over to lick it cautiously round the inside.

John Burns would climb the ladder and ask him to play football.

'I'll be out as soon as I get this eker done,' Colm would answer. But hearing the ball bounce on the waste ground and John shouting: 'Let her come!' he would close his books quickly, run out to his companions, and play football until dark.

With the coming of June, riots broke out once more. A special police force was recruited from the Orange Order, and on his way to school Colm could see them in their cage-cars or standing at street corners with their rifles, canvas bandoliers, and rough black-green uniforms.

'Them's our Black-and-Tans,' he heard a shawled woman shout at them. 'It's a poor show and little sleep we'll get on the Falls Road now!'

Not a day passed in peace, and as Colm played on the waste ground he could hear the shots shattering the summer air, and was thankful that his street was sheltered and away from it all. It was strange to be living in a city where night after night shots rang out and to know nothing of what happened until they read the morning's paper. It was strange, too, to be leaving their game of football when it was still bright and to retire to their houses because of curfew.

But the hours of curfew were not peaceful. From early morning the snipers were at their posts and they did not cease with the coming of curfew and the bare streets.

And there came a Saturday evening when Alec, because of the sniping, could not venture out of the house to get down to Mrs Heaney's, and while he was asleep with Colm and Jamesy their mother came into the room and wakened them. It was about two in the morning and dark.

'Alec!' she said. 'Come into the front room till you hear the shouts and screams. There's something queer going on.'

Alec got up at once and Colm and Jamesy followed him to their mother's room. Outside they could hear, far away, screams and shouts and the blowing of whistles, and when Alec pulled down the window to listen the noise was louder and stronger.

'Where would that be?' his mother asked.

'It'd be the streets around the Monastery,' he replied, looking out upon his own street, cold and quiet under the light from the lamps.

Colm and Jamesy shivered; they felt empty and faint as they heard the murderous screams in the night air. They began to talk to Alec.

'Whisht, will ye,' he said to them, 'till I hear what's wrong!'

Other streets were taking up the cries, adding to the wild turmoil.

'Somebody must be getting murdered, Alec,' the mother put in and turned to Clare who was sitting up in bed, wide awake and terrified.

In the neighbouring street the dogs began to bark and the people to shout. 'Murder! Murder! Murder!' Now it had reached their own street; windows were pulled down and women started to scream. Downstairs Rover barked.

'Mammy, Mammy, I'm sick!' and Clare leaned out of the bed and retched on the floor.

A scream broke from the mother: 'Oh, God! Why did we ever come to this town! Alec, for God's sake, give up this fight for Ireland! Holy Mother of God, I can't stand it any longer!'

'Is that the way for an Irish mother to talk?' Alec blazed. 'Where would Ireland be if mothers talked like that? Do you want us to be like them spineless Hibernians, afraid to talk to you in the street for fear their houses would be raided and their sons arrested? . . . Whisht!'

Neighbours were out in the street now; Alec went downstairs in his shirt and trousers. Men and women were standing at their doors.

'What's up? What's wrong?' all were asking, but nobody could give an answer.

And then when they heard the rattle of a patrol lorry they all rushed into their houses and waited for the commotion to die down. They went to bed, but not to sleep, wondering what had happened and waiting for the blessed daylight.

Alec went to an early Mass, and when he came back his face was saddened with grief. Colm and Jamesy met him at the foot of the street. His boots were wet and covered with clay.

'I was up seeing a poor fellow that was dragged from his bed last night and murdered. He's lying at the side of a lonin away beyond the brickfields. Don't be going up near it!' he said to them.

They waited until he went into the house and then made off up through the fields. A few people had gathered around the murdered man as he lay stretched on the roadside, and above them was the mountain with its top covered with morning mist. Colm and Jamesy ran over to the knot of people and looked sadly at the dead man. His friends, when they had found him, put boots on his feet and they were unlaced; a navy blue coat was on him, a gilt cross pinned in the lapel; his hair was wet, a red gash at the side of his mouth, and his hands joined.

At Mass that morning Colm could not rid his mind of the dead man and he offered up prayers for him. At night he often called out in his sleep and, if Alec weren't there, his mother would steal into the room to find him in a hot sweat.

There came more nights of terror, but towards the end of that month of June a lull came as the King and Queen of England opened the Belfast Parliament and Ireland was partitioned.

Colm sat for exams in the College. Then came July and the summer holidays, but there was no peace. Houses were raided by police and auxiliaries during curfew; and in the poorer Catholic districts the people were organised to raise the cry of 'Murder! Murder!' if anyone entered their streets at night.

One night a lorry load of police and specials was ambushed by the Republicans in Raglan Street. One policeman was shot dead and some wounded.

Sitting up in their beds the MacNeills heard the volleys of shots crackling like breaking sticks. Colm was the only one who knew that Alec was out with the Republicans, for that evening he had told him as he gave him his pocket-book and asked him to pray. Now as he listened with cold fear to the air alive with shots he couldn't pray; he thought of Alec with a light rifle at his shoulder firing from the cover of an entry or from behind a lamp-post.

His mother had her beads in one hand and with the other was keeping the bed-clothes over Clare's head. But the ferocious din would have wakened the dead, and the whole night long it continued and even into the growing day.

Four weeks of Colm's holidays had passed before peace came to the city and hovered over it like a spring cloud. Women wheeled out their prams and went up to the park; and one Saturday afternoon Alec, Colm, Jamesy, and Rover went up the fields to the mountain. Jamesy had a long pair of flannel trousers on him, tubular and oil-stained, and carried in one of the pockets a bottle of milk which was corked with a wad of twisted paper. Colm had sandwiches made from tinned meat, and Alec had bought apples and a packet of cigarettes for himself.

It was a lovely day with the sun shining and people stretched in the fields. Up past the brickyard they went, looking down at the deep pit, and clay hard and caked, the bogie lines shining. Into the wide open fields they raced where Rover rolled over and over with delight and barked teasingly at Colm and Jamesy. They jumped a little stream and came out of the fields on to the White Rock Road. At the top of it an ice-cream man was sitting on the shaft of his red-painted barrow. Alec bought three sliders from him and they sucked them as they climbed the white stony lonin that led to the mountain's foot.

Banks and hedges were at each side and filled the lonin with leaf-shadow and a dewy coolness. Here and there were crumpled newspapers where lovers had crushed into the banks the previous night. On big boulders there was printed in white paint: WHAT THINK YE OF CHRIST? ALL HAVE SINNED.

At gaps in the hedges they stood to look down at the city and felt the blood hammering in their heads. Alec loosed his belt, and Rover lay in a stream that swirled over stones at the side of the lonin. They passed a lake with a line of pines, and a tin church – so small and so diminutive that it looked like a child's toy. And then they reached the foot of the mountain, Alec puffing and blowing: 'Thank God, we're here at last!'

He sat down on the bank near the drinking pool and fanned himself with his cap. 'I'll have a quare slug of that in a few minutes,' he said to himself as he watched Colm and Jamesy put their mouths to the cold spurt of water that gushed into the pool. Rover rolled his liver-and-white body in it while Colm and Jamesy splashed it around their hot faces and plastered their hair.

Their path cut diagonally up the mountain. It was loose and stony, and the heat struck up from it in thick waves. Colm and Jamesy led the way, and Alec stopped often to admire the view. Jamesy hurled a stone down the side and heard it bumping until it fell and broke in pieces at the bottom. Colm lifted a brown caterpillar that was crossing the path and placed it on the palm of his hand, counting the rings on its back whenever it stretched itself.

At the top of the mountain they lay in the heather and gazed at Belfast spread out in the flat hollow below them, its lean mill chimneys stretched above the haze of smoke. Rows of red-bricked houses radiated on all sides and above them rose blocks of factories with many of their windows catching the sunlight.

They saw their own street and could make out the splash of whitewash on the wall that Alec had daubed there as a mark for his pigeons; it was all very far away like a street seen through the wrong end of a telescope.

'I can see my mother standing at the back-door throwing a crust to the fowl and Biddy McAteer hanging out her curtains,' joked Jamesy.

'And look at Mrs O'Brien cleaning her ear with a knitting needle,' answered Colm.

Alec gave a loud sniff: 'Man dear, I can smell the sausages frying for our tea.'

Their eyes ranged over the whole city to the low ridge of the Castlereagh Hills, netted with lovely fields and skimming cloud-shadows, to the blue U-shaped lough covered with yachts as small as paper boats, and steamers moving up towards the docks where the gantries stood like poised aeroplanes.

They shouted out to each other the names of all the churches that they knew: there were the green spires of Ardoyne where the sinners brought their great sins to the Passionists, there was the stumpy spire of the Monastery, and farther along in the heart of the city, sticking high above the smoke, were the sharp spires of St Peter's – the church that was always crowded with shawled factory workers saying their beads. Near their own street was the Dominican Convent, its fields very green and its hockey posts very white. And when Jamesy asked was it true that the nuns dug a bit of their graves each day and slept in their coffins at night Alec laughed: 'It'd be a queer deep grave some of them ladies would have for they're as ould as the hills.'

The numerous spires of the Protestant churches were everywhere. Then there was the Falls Park and they could see people walking about in it, and below it Celtic Football ground with its oval field and one grand stand, and farther to the right Linfield ground with its tin advertisements for cigarettes.

'Wouldn't you think now to see all the churches,' smiled Alec, 'and all the factories and playgrounds that it was a Christian town?' and he lay back in the heather, flung his arms wide, and laughed.

They saw his great chest heaving as he drew in deep breaths of the air.

'Man, but that's a glorious day!' he said from his heart.

'But how long will all this peace last?'

Rover panted beside him. Butterflies opened and closed their wings on the heather. Larks tried to burst their throats in song and Colm, lying back, tried to find them, but the blue of the sky stung his eyes. He sat up and told Jamesy that it was time to pass round the milk.

Alec divided the sandwiches; Jamesy pulled the wad of milk-blackened paper from the neck of the bottle, took a drink, and handed it to Colm.

The noise of the city came up to them; they heard a train whistle and saw its white fluttering scarf of smoke above the houses, burrowing through trees, rush past the Bog Meadows smashed with pools of water, and out into the quietude of the open fields.

They got up and walked along the mountain's ridge into wild bare country. A cool breeze rushed at them.

'Fill your lungs with that!' said Alec. 'That's as good as the Rathlin air any day. It has come over Lough Neagh as clean and fresh as a spring well.'

Colm thought of the wind coming over Rathlin, shaking the grass on the top of the empty house, bounding over black Knocklayde, bumping through villages, ruffling Lough Neagh, and sweeping up to the mountain where they were now.

Alec stood with outstretched arms and inhaled loudly, the buttons almost bursting on his waistcoat, his face red, and the wind tossing his fair hair. Across a black stream he lifted Colm and Jamesy, one in each arm. Then they began to run and trip each other in the wiry grass – Rover barking at them and sniffing at fern tufts for rabbits.

Once they stopped to look back at the city which would soon disappear from view, and Alec held Colm and Jamesy tightly and pointed to Cave Hill with sun shining on it.

'Do you see that hill?' he said to them. 'Over a hundred years ago great patriots stood on it and looked down at

Belfast; they were Wolfe Tone, Henry Joy McCracken, Neilson and some others whose names I forget – anyway they were all Protestants. And do you know what they swore? They took an oath that they'd never rest quietly in their graves till the authority of England over this country was overthrown and our independence achieved ... But that spirit has gone from amongst all of them except a few, scattered to nothingness within a hundred years.' He swept his hand towards the city: 'There they are below us now, a race of people living in a land that they do not serve!'

'And will they ever come to love Ireland again?' Colm asked.

'That's a poser,' smiled Alec. 'It's like asking us to march at the Twelfth of July. It will come, but not in our time ... Till then we must thole all; to give in would be as cowardly as suicide!'

Rover barked and they turned to see him rush into a clump of bracken and a rabbit race madly up the mountain side. They all ran after it, whistling and shouting, but Rover didn't see it as he raced excitedly hither and thither with his nose to the ground. Presently they reached the mountain quarries. Below them was the humped-back County of Down with its yellow wheat fields, rings of trees, and on the sky line the lovely triangular mountains of Mourne.

The mountain slope merged into Hannastown and they hurried down on to the road. They called in the brown-gloomed mountainy church. Inside was a musty smell of decay, damp oozing from the walls, and two candles burning before a picture of Our Lady. They knelt in different seats, their whispered prayers sounding as loud as wind in grass.

Out again they came for the long walk home. Alec cut sticks for them in a hedge, and Colm and Jamesy whacked the heads of all the dandelions that grew along the banks. Down the White Rock Road they went, past the Gaelic ground, and saw boys with hurley sticks and paper parcels march from it, whistling and singing. At the City Cemetery gate they saw crowds of Protestants coming out after tending their graves all day.

At home Clare had an apron on and was washing the floor. She cried when Rover ran across it with his dirty paws. She swiped at him with the floor cloth, and he scrambled under the sofa and lay on his forepaws, looking at her with mild eyes. She spread newspapers on it to keep it clean; and when the mother came in with lettuce for the tea the boys cheered.

SIXTEEN

When Colm went back to the school at the beginning of September, Father Daly told him that he had passed his examination, though he had done badly in Mathematics. Next year he could matriculate or cram for the King's Scholarship Examination, in which case, says Father Daly: 'You'd have to do Drawing, Spellings, Penmanship, Tonic sol-fa, and learn by heart a play of Shakespeare's and one-hundred-and-sixty-five lines of poetry. The questions on the prescribed play are always the same: "By whom, to whom, and on what occasion were the so-and-so words spoken", and in the questions on poetry all you've got to do is to supply missing lines in given stanzas. Wouldn't you like that?' He seemed to say all this with a kind of serious smile and Colm was bewildered.

That week he had a letter from Father Byrne telling him to work hard in his last year at the College and advising him to sit for the King's Scholarship Examination and become a teacher; he also enclosed five shillings.

When Saturday came Colm brought Clare to the pictures, and afterwards took her to the bird-shops to see the mice in the lighted windows revolving on a wheel. A white rabbit with pink eyes hung outside in a wired box. Colm lifted Clare in his arms to see it, and she put her finger at the mesh and jumped with delighted excitement when the rabbit sniffed at it. He bought her two goldfish in a glass bowl and then passed into Smithfield where he spent his last twopence at a machine that showed a house going on fire and little mechanical men racing up a ladder and saving a girl from a smoke-enveloped window.

'That's not real smoke, Colm; isn't it only wadding?' said Clare; and she asked him questions that he couldn't answer and he was glad when they reached a toy stall where the dolls completely captured her mind. She admired most a little Japanese doll that had a fringe of real hair, but when she put her finger in the doll's eyes the stall-owner glared at her.

'If you're not going to buy, keep your hands to yourself!' she scolded, and propped the doll against a toy horse.

Clare blushed and took Colm's hand, and together they moved out of Smithfield on to the road for home, watching regretfully the lighted trams race past them. Now and again they would stop when Clare wanted to look at the goldfish to see if they were still alive. The brown paper that covered the bowl was now wet and it was easy to tear a peep-hole at the side.

The mother was standing at the door waiting for them when they reached the street, and Clare ran to tell her about the goldfish.

The kitchen was clean and warm, the fender glittering with black-lead, and smoothed shirts and collars hanging stiff from the line. The glass globe of the gas had just been washed and the light was now unusually bright.

Colm put the goldfish on the table and when he peeled off the damp paper the fish swirled round and round the bowl sending shining bubbles to the top.

'Put them in the scullery; they're cross with the gaslight,' suggested the mother.

'What makes them look so big, Colm?' Clare asked.

'The glass is magnified,' he remarked emphatically, though he didn't know whether it was or not. He put the bowl on a shelf in the scullery and told Clare not to forget to change the water every day.

The mother rinsed out the teapot, Clare placed cups on the table, and Rover rubbed his side against Colm's legs. He scratched the dog on the top of the head and laughed at the way the left hind leg beat rapidly on the floor.

'He likes that!' said the mother, putting water into the teapot.

Colm covered his face with his hands and pretended to cry. Rover licked him and began to whine.

'Ah, Colm, don't tease him,' Clare pleaded.

At nine o'clock Jamesy came in. His face was dirty, his long trousers white with flour, and his wages in his fist. He handed six shillings and sixpence to his mother.

'I kept one and a tanner this week for I'm saving up to buy two White Beveren rabbits.'

' 'Deed you're ill off for rabbits! And with Clare's goldfish we may start a menagerie anytime!' smiled the mother.

She counted the money in her hand and gave a shilling to Colm.

'That'll do you for tram money for a whole week and when it's done, don't be asking for any more.'

Colm laughed: 'It's well we have somebody toiling or we'd be out in the street.'

Jamesy shouted from the scullery where he was washing, 'We're a quare while waiting for you to earn money, Mister Smarty!'

Colm was going to reply when his mother put her finger on her lips, beckoning him to be quiet.

Jamesy came into the kitchen with a towel in his hands, his ears covered with soap. Colm smiled: 'Was it snowing when you came in?'

Jamesy didn't answer him, but instinctively the towel went to his ears, and he rubbed them briskly.

The mother opened the oven-door, gripped two sandwiched plates with the corner of her apron, and placed them on the table for Jamesy. She lifted off the top plate and there arose a smell of onions and fried steak.

'Aw, Mammy,' coaxed Clare, 'I'd like a bit of that!'

'You got your share; it's for somebody that's been working hard and sore all day.'

When the meal was finished and the dishes cleared away Colm and Jamesy dressed Rover in a coat and cap and tied a blue ribbon round his neck. They lifted him up to let him see himself in the looking-glass and just before curfew Alec came in and, seeing the dress-up of Rover, turned his back to the dog and asked: 'Where's Rover? Did any of you see Rover about? Where is the poor fella?'

He looked in the scullery and opened the coalhouse door. 'I wonder where he is?'

Rover followed, trying to stand in front of Alec, but Alec always edged away from him. At last Rover tore at the cap and ribbon with his paws, sat back on his haunches, wagged his tail and barked.

'Och, there he is,' says Alec, turning round and lifting the dog in his arms. 'My great big fella! My great big fella!'

When Alec had settled himself on the sofa, Clare, Jamesy, and Colm watched him expectantly. A banana was pointed revolver-like at Jamesy, an apple thrown to Clare and one to Colm, and for his mother some dates in a paper bag.

They sat for a while quietly and Alec looked through the evening's paper.

'You'll be safe enough stopping here the night?' asked the mother.

'Certainly, they seemed to have stopped arresting. The internment camps must be full,' Alec replied as he scanned the paper.

'All quiet down town?' she continued – her usual question for the past two years.

'There's not a cheep anywhere and the town was packed tonight.'

The five of them knelt for the rosary and each gave out a decade, the others answering. They turned out the gas and said it in the firelight. The broken pictures glinted in the light and distracted Colm for his mind wandered away from the prayers, back to the night when the house was raided, and he kept wondering when Alec was going to get new glass in them.

The rosary was soon over and Colm realised that his prayers had been spoiled. He slipped up to the room before Alec and Jamesy and tried to make amends by saying a few prayers at his bedside. He heard Alec bolt the scullery door and saw the light leave the yard. He was on his feet when Alec and Jamesy came into the room.

It was very still. Handkerchiefs hung limp and cold from the quiet line in the yard. A shunting train far away by the Bog Meadows sounded near.

'It's a long time since I remember so still a night,' Alec said as he got into bed.

Clare coughed a few times in the other room and listening to her Colm lived again in his mind their visit to the bird-shop while down in the scullery shelf the goldfish, silent as the night, moved round and round in their glass bowl . . .

Far away Rover was barking; then somewhere, sometime, his mother hovered over the bed shaking him and Alec. He opened his eyes.

'Alec, Alec! Waken up!' his mother was saying in a

frightened voice. 'There's a bunch of men at the door and I don't like the look of them!'

Alec got out of bed and pulled on his trousers. Colm followed him.

The door was knocked, but not loudly.

Alec looked out of the window. The place was in darkness except for the handkerchiefs swaying coldly on the line.

'They're going to arrest me!'

'God help us, maybe they're only coming to search the house!'

Rover growled as the knock came again.

'I'll open it, Mother!' Alec raised his voice.

He passed downstairs, the mother and Colm leaning over the banisters.

'Lie down! Lie down there!' Alec was saying to the dog, and his voice came clear up the little stairs.

And then the door opened. There was a stumble. Shots cracked and split the air. The mother screamed and ran downstairs.

In the hallway Alec lay. His shirt was wet with blood. She lifted his head and clasped it in her two hands: 'The priest! The priest!'

Colm ran out through the open door in his bare feet. Around him people were screaming from the closed houses: 'Murder! Murder!' Near a lamp-post he saw Rover lying on his side, dark slimy blood oozing across the pavement. He ran past it, down the street, round the corner and on to the main road with its lighted lamps and shining tramlines.

His bare feet thudded on the pavement and made a pinging sound as he passed corrugated railings. Up the hill he ran and then at the corner of a street two black figures jumped out to meet him, but he swerved and ran past them, harder and harder. Behind him he heard them shout: 'Halt! Halt!' and it echoed and re-echoed in the night air. They shouted again, but he didn't stop. There were shots and their noise filled up the whole world and resounded from the empty road. But Colm found himself going on. Then he turned the corner of the convent grounds with its black granite walls and came in sight of the church. A lamp with a broken mantle blinked and snored, and a bullet whined.

In through the open gate and up the stone steps of the presbytery he ran, pounding at the door with his fists, looking round to see if he were pursued. His eyes bulged; his mouth was open and his breath scorched his throat. He heard someone moving; a window was lifted up and someone looked out. Colm felt his knees melt from under him, and when the door opened he fell in a faint in the hall ... Two priests bent over him, bathing his forehead with ice-cold water. They gave him brandy off a spoon. Slowly his senses gathered and he was able to tell them what had happened.

His teeth chattered madly and his forehead tingled in a cold, cold sweat. The priests wound a thick scarf round his neck, and taking him by the hand they walked quietly down a long street and out across the fields – a short cut to the house. The fields were dark, the sky black and filled with stars. A single light shone in a shed of the brick-works and an engine throbbed slowly.

With difficulty they found the cinder path and one of the priests carried Colm on his back over the rough cinders. The crunch of cinders, the smell of hair oil from the priest's hair, the blackness of the night, and the remembrance of the blood blended in Colm's mind, and he trembled, cried, and laughed hysterically.

They came out from the fields to the first street lamp and heard people talking. Women were crying at their doors; men in their shirt sleeves stood in groups; they had broken the rule of curfew.

There was a large patch of blood underneath one of the

lamps, but Rover was gone. The people around the door made way for the priests. 'He's dead, Father! He's dead!' they were saying, and cries arose in the air.

In the light of the kitchen Alec lay stretched on the sofa, his shirt red with blood, his eyes closed in death. His mother was crying: 'My poor, poor son!' Blood dripped on to the floor. One of the priests bent over the body and the people began to pray.

Mrs Tully took Colm into her house: 'Bear up, son.' As she passed the people at the door she cried: 'It's well for them that gets away young – they don't have the suffering of growing old.'

Theresa and Joe Heaney arrived from England the morning of the funeral.

In the parlour Alec lay in his coffin. Women crowded the kitchen and men sat on the stairs waiting for the priest. The sunlight flowed in soft gold through the blind-drawn window and there was the shuffling of feet outside as people gathered for the funeral.

Presently the priest entered the house and the people knelt down when he kissed his purple stole and put it round his neck. The sunlight bronzed his face as he recited the prayers and a sickly wine smell came from the wood of the coffin. The corpse was sprinkled with Holy Water and before the lid was put on, the mother, Theresa, Colm, Jamesy, and Clare took their leave of Alec, kissing the dead face and bursting into tears.

The green, white, and gold flag of Ireland was thrown over the coffin, but when it was carried out to the street policemen rushed across and snatched the flag. A smothered groan arose from the people and a girl shouted: 'Are ye not satisfied with murderin' him that ye won't let us bury him in peace!'

That night Alec's comrades stole into the graveyard and fired three volleys over his grave.

SEVENTEEN

A few days after the funeral Theresa, Joe, and their baby returned to England, and Mrs Heaney stayed awhile with the MacNeills to keep them company. In the mornings she arose early, lit the fire, and brought a cup of tea up to the mother. Jamesy went to his work; Colm got into the bakery as a clerk; and Clare stopped from school to run messages.

Then the mother got a few hours' work as charwoman in the parish chapel. She hadn't to start work until ten o'clock and when she had made the breakfast she always hurried out to hear the nine o'clock Mass.

During her first day in the church she was scrubbing vigorously in the aisle when a young curate, fresh from college and full of self-importance, rebuked her for working in the presence of the Blessed Sacrament without her hat on.

'But, Father,' she had replied, her face ablaze with shame,

'I didn't know it was wrong.'

'You didn't know it was wrong! What kind of a school did you go to!' and he walked away, leaving her standing in the half-washed aisle.

She put on her hat and returned to her work. People came in, said a few prayers, genuflected and went out. Her hands were unsteady and she felt weak, ashamed, and agonised; but she'd say nothing to Colm and Jamesy. And that night she laughed about the fleas she has seen in the dust and how the poor priests must be ate alive in the confessionals.

'I declare to God,' she said, 'I saw a flea as big as a horse.'

Colm shrugged his shoulders and she smiled timidly at him: 'Och, sure a flea's a clean thing and they'll always be about where you get a lock of people.'

They were glad to hear her talk light-heartedly again; but all the time her mind was filled with the scolding from the priest, and when she went to bed she cried secretly on the pillow.

The following evening when Jamesy and Colm were ready to go out Mrs Heaney arrived in great haste. It was Colm who opened the door for her and she walked in quickly.

'Now, now, where's your mother, Colm? Where is she?' and she could hardly get the words out with excitement.

'She's making the beds,' he said, and she plunged up the stairs, calling out, 'Mary, are you there?' Are you there, Mary?'

They listened at the foot of the stairs and heard the creak of a bed as she plopped down on it.

'Now, now, sit down a minute, Mary, till I get my breath ... Good news.'

She mumbled something that they couldn't hear so they walked up the stairs and into the room. She was sitting on the bed holding Mrs MacNeill's two hands in her own as she told her about the American White Cross Fund.

'And you'll be entitled to so much a week for yourself and so much for each child,' she was saying. 'And Colm will fill in the form right now. Better get in at once for dear knows how long the money will last. I know a fella in the White Cross Office and he'll see that ye get your share. Don't you worry, Mary, every thing will be all right. There's a woman in our street and her man's workin' and her son's in jail for being in the IRA. And do ye know how much she's gettin' from the White Cross for that son? Fifteen shillings a week! – and the same boy, let me tell you, never earned a penny piece in his life ... Ah, Mary, our cow'll soon calve and then Jamesy'll give us the 'Turf Man'.'

A short time afterwards the MacNeills were getting a guinea a week from the White Cross, and what with Jamesy's eight shillings and Colm's fifteen they were able, as the mother said, 'to make ends meet'. Often she thought of Colm and wished that he could have continued at the College, but Mrs Heaney would always say: 'Now, now, daughter, don't talk like that! Let well enough alone. He's happy in the bakery. He's sure of that job and, God knows, he might be manager some day!'

Colm was always the first to arrive at the bakery office in the morning. He was in long trousers now and with his hands in his pockets, a skull cap on his head, his boots well-polished, and the smell of soap fresh on his face, he would wait for the manager to come with the keys. He would wander into the yard to watch the bread-servers brush and tackle their horses, but when the hot doughy smell drifted from the bake-house it reminded him of Alec and he would hurry out of the yard.

Once inside the office he would get ready the long order-sheets, neatly write the bread-servers' names on them, and calculate in pounds, shillings, and pence the amount of bread issued:

TICKETS

2lb Plain
2lb Turnovers
2lb Open Pan
2lb Wheaten Pan
2lb Crusty
2lb Lodger Loaves
2lb Torpedo

A long list of names of pastry, scones, and fancy loaves followed and in his slack periods he often amused himself by combining the initial letters into Rathlin place-names. And one day the manager, seeing these names cryptically written down on a sheet of paper, thought they were names of racehorses, and, without preface, lectured Colm on the evils of gambling. Colm couldn't understand why he should talk to him about gambling and then one morning, the day of the November handicap, one of the bread-servers met him outside the office.

'Colm!' said he. 'What'll win the Big One?'

'The Big what?'

'Don't pretend you're soft. Didn't the boss tell us that you're a demon at the horses. He told us that there's not a bloody nag in Ireland or England that you don't know its breeding, its form, and its prospects. We all know you! And I believe you're workin' out a code system ... You're a soft lad, all right. And to look at you you'd think butter wouldn't melt in yer mouth!'

Colm laughed at him: 'I don't know what you're talking about.'

'G'long,' said the bread-server, getting angry. 'You wouldn't think you were a brother of Alec's ... Ye can keep your tips and your code, and to hell with the whole lot of them!'

Colm wondered was he making game of him and many a

time he wanted to ask the manager about the racehorses, but shyness always overcame him. Christmas approached and in the rush of orders for the bakery and his working late at night, the incident was soon forgotten.

His mother, too, had advised him not to speak too much to his manager, for Jamesy, a few days before Christmas, had asked for a rise and Mr McGrath gave him the sack: 'I just thought you were getting too cocky of late, talking to me as if I were your uncle. So when you're discontented you can go.'

'It's a bad thing,' the mother advised, 'to get too friendly with your boss. They don't like you to talk too much to them. Colm, speak to your manager only when he speaks to you ... It's a pity, Jamesy, you'll not get all the Christmas boxes and you after running the messages all the year.'

Jamesy had plenty of time to himself now and, out of an old soap box, he began to make a Christmas crib for Clare. It was to be a surprise for her and he worked at it in the pigeon-shed. He talked about putting a battery and an electric star in it, but when Christmas Eve arrived it still remained a plain box. He searched about for a brush and paint, but the arrival of a football, a present from Joe, made him relinquish the task with the excuse: 'The poorer a crib looks, the better the crib! There wasn't much paint about the Cave at Bethlehem, I bet you!'

Colm was off at three o'clock and all that evening before the fall of dark they played with the ball out on the mud-soft waste ground. A black wind skimmed over the field, hurled itself at the palings, and blew through the wintry trees in McCrea's.

The mother came to the back-door, a plate in her hand, and scraped the crumbs from it for the birds. Through the trees she saw the lights of a tram going up the hill, and when she heard the thump of the ball in the dark air she called to them.

'We're going now, Mother,' they shouted, and when they looked across at the back of the houses they saw wedges of light above every yard-wall. Darkness had come.

They came into the yard, their boots heavy with mud, and Jamesy carrying the ball by the lace. The light from the kitchen shone out to them; it shone on the white-washed walls, on the water in the grate and on the red berries of a holly-bush lying in the corner.

'Playing out in the dark like two fools and maybe get your end,' the mother said to them.

Their faces were red and mud-streaked.

'We're roasting!' they assured her.

'Don't plough across the clean floor with them clabbery boots,' and she handed them a newspaper and a knife with a broken blade.

They scraped off the dirt, and from a piece of mud flung on the yard there emerged a worm, its wet body gleaming in the light. Colm watched it as it wriggled and stretched across the blue tiles, and caught Jamesy's hand when he wanted to sever it with the knife.

'It's bad luck to cut a worm in two; it'll bring on the rain!'

'That's a yarn and a half! I never believed it; wait now till I prove it,' and he stooped over the worm with the knife poised.

'Och, Jamesy, give it a chance for its life, tomorrow's Christmas,' and he smiled as Jamesy straightened himself and cleaned the knife with his finger.

They came into the warmth of the clean kitchen. Their mother was in black, pouring out the tea.

'The two of you get out to Confession early and don't be leaving everything to the last minute ... What Mass are yez for in the morning?'

'I'm for six,' replied Colm.

'And you, lazy bones?'

'Ten will do me rightly!' Jamesy answered.

When they had finished the tea Jamesy went upstairs and placed Clare's crib on top of a brown trunk on the landing. He lit a stump of a candle and lifted up the loose cloth tacked in front of the box. The light shone into it. On the yellow straw lay a delft Child with outstretched hands and beside Him stood two pieces of cardboard with coloured pictures of Our Lady and Saint Joseph pasted on to them.

He called to his mother and Colm. Colm asked about the electric light that was to adorn it, but Jamesy pretended not to hear him. The mother with her hands across her breast said it was lovely and promised not to say a word about it to Clare, and from her purse she gave him a shilling to buy a frosted globe and a night light for it.

They went out together and called into St Paul's for Confession, but the church was packed, and they came out again and hurried to St Peter's, but it, too, was crowded with penitents, and they walked to St Mary's.

'I'll tell you what we'll do,' suggested Colm. 'We'll go round to see the shops first and, maybe, when we come back the crowd will have lessened.'

Down High Street they went and stood for a while at Robb's to see the toys and a train with electric lights race round the window; then into North Street where crowds thronged the pavements and the road. Handcarts were piled with fruit and hawkers shouted: 'Bananas 6d a dozen ... Tomatoes, 5d a pound!' and all the time they stamped their feet to keep themselves warm.

Outside Woolworth's a man had a pole with large coloured balloons nodding at the top of it. Beside him was Father Christmas dressed in a long red coat with a mud-spattered tail, a false face, and a wooden tray of mechanical toys strapped to his chest. Now and again he would wind up one of his toy men, place it on the pavement, and watch it as it walked round and round. Once the little man walked too far and fell over the kerb, his legs working rapidly and the spring buzzing.

'It's a good horse that doesn't stumble. Accidents happen to us all! ... Sixpence for the dancing man! ... The real McCoy for a Christmas stocking! ... And look what we have for the girls.' And he took out from a deep pocket a naked celluloid doll with black, coquettish eyes.

Jamesy counted the pennies in his pocket without taking them out; he wondered should he buy one for Clare.

'Only a few more left,' Father Christmas was saying as he adjusted the chin of his false face.

A policeman came over and spoke to him. Father Christmas still kept on his false face and his dark eyes looked nervously from side to side.

'Do you hear what I asked you? Have you a hawker's licence?'

Through the mouth–hole of the false face Colm saw Father Christmas wet his lips.

A crowd had gathered and the lights from Woolworth's shone out on them.

The policeman took out his note book: 'If you don't give me your name and address I'll be compelled to take you to the barracks.'

'Ma!' said a little boy. 'Is he goin' till arrest Daddy Christmas?'

''Deed, sowl, he's not!' she shouted.

The policeman turned to her and his face was red. Other women with black shawls over their heads began to shout: 'He's tryin' to earn an honest penny ... Lave him alone! ... Don't go with him! ... Well dar' you arrest him!'

Father Christmas began to plead from behind the cover of his false face. The policeman gripped him by the arm; there was a stumble and the tray of toys spilled on to the kerb. The women cursed and pressed closer to the policeman. One woman thumped him with her fists on the back and in the excitement Father Christmas wrenched himself free and with his coat-tails flying he made up Garfield Street, a line of celluloid dolls and mechanical men falling from his pockets.

Crowds here and there stood to cheer the runaway Father Christmas as he dodged through the traffic and hid himself in the dark narrow streets around Smithfield.

Jamesy lifted one of the dolls. 'What'll I do with it, Colm?'

'Keep it. God knows where Father Christmas is by this time.'

'But will I have to tell it in Confession?'

'The priest will have a quare laugh to himself if you tell him the whole story.'

They passed out of North Street; Salvation Army groups were rattling tambourines and singing Christmas hymns. Farther along a youth was standing on a platform and women with saddened eyes were gathered around him. He was telling them how he first saw the 'Light'. Sweat gleamed on his forehead and his voice became husky with sincerity: 'Come to Christ, all of ye. How sweet and tender are his words! He stretches out His hand from the Cross on this Christmas Eve to you all. Stop and listen to Him. Stop and shake His hand. Think of Time! Think of Eternity and the Lake of Fire. Time shall cease and Eternity shall go on and on . . .'

Near him a circle of people were gathered around a black man who was assuring them that he would remove their corns with one application of his ointment: 'You can't have a happy Christmas with sore feet. Put the ointment on overnight. See!' and he stretches out his long black wrist, twirls his little finger inside a box of his ointment and rubs it on one of his knuckles. 'Clean it off in the morning and your corn is lifted out as clean as an egg from an egg-cup . . . Only sixpence!'

A man in tram-conductor's uniform and an empty

lemonade box under his arm suddenly put the box on the ground and stood upon it. He began to address the crowd around the black man and they all flocked towards him.

'I'm a sincere workin' man,' he orated. 'I grudge nobody his bite of bread as long as he gets it without suckin' the blood from the poor. If he's a workin' man he's a friend of mine whether he's a Protestant, a Catholic, or a Jew. We are all workers – tryin' to live and let live; that's my policy. But is it the policy of this town? Is it? Who does the riotin' and the fightin'? Look at the lists of dead and wounded these days in the papers. What d'ye see? They are all the names of workers – all workin' people! Ye never seen shootin' in the Malone Road or Balmoral or in the other flashy districts of this town. I suppose it puts them off their sleep when they hear the shots bein' carried to them by the wind. And Lady Duff would turn to Master Harold and say: "There's that beastly shooting again. They are impossible people in this city! Impossible! Harold, get up and close the window." And Harold would laugh and scratch himself against his silk pyjamas. And maybe at that moment an ould woman – a rickle of bones – is shot dead in York Street. And what's Harold thinkin' about – Keep them at it! Keep the workers at one another's throats and they'll forget about high rents and low wages ...' The orator jumped off his box and with his two hands stretched above his head he yelled: 'Yez are all mugs in this town! All mugs! Listen to this, brothers! Supposin' ye got all the Orange sashes and all the Green sashes in this town and ye tied them around loaves of bread and flung them over Queen's Bridge, what would happen? ... What would happen? ... The gulls – the gulls that fly in the air, what would they do? They'd go for the bread! But *you* – the other Gulls – would go for the sashes every time! ...'

Everyone laughed. The orator got up on his box again. Colm and Jamesy shivered and snuffled with the cold and moved off briskly to St Mary's. The confessionals were still crowded, and they took the tram to the Passionists at Ardoyne. Up, up the tram climbed, away from the noise of the city's centre, up to the dark windy streets clustered around the high church.

Colm led the way to a confession box that had few people seated close to it. Jamesy hesitated: 'He might be a cross man when there's not many going to him.'

'If he sends you back to North Street with the doll what'll you do?' joked Colm.

After Confession they were light-hearted and they walked across the Shankill Road towards home. The sky was black and cold. Lights were lit in all the little houses and needles of frost were glinting on the road. From every pub came the noisy chatter of arguing men, and outside one of them a man was standing in the street, his bare toes sticking out of his boots and his ragged clothes hanging loosely upon him. Jamesy recognised him as a street-singer he had seen often on the Falls Road.

He was now singing in a loud, raucous voice:

> When William's cannon roared aloud,
>   Their thunder winged by fate,
> When rose our Constitution proud
>   In sixteen eighty-eight;
> When it, upon destruction's brink,
>   Our sires led on the van,
> That's another reason fair, I think,
>   Why I'm an Orangeman.
>
> To guard that faith that like the sun
>   Is not of this world's light,
> To guard our Constitution, won
>   At Boyne's immortal fight.
> To purify from Popery's sink,
>   To check rebellion's clan,

> These are other reasons fair, I think,
> Why I'm an Orangeman.

'Do you know,' said Jamesy when the man had finished, 'I heard him singing 'Wrap the Green Flag Round Me' on the Falls Road.'

'S-s-sh,' Colm hushed. 'He might hear you and get us chased.'

They hurried away from him and when Jamesy turned to look back he saw two drunk men bringing the singer into the pub.

When they got home their mother was cleaning the duck, and a plum-pudding was bumping in a pot on the fire for the morrow's dinner. Clare was chopping an onion and her eyes were watering. Jamesy slipped up stairs with his green-frosted lamp and lit it at the crib; in the morning Clare would be delighted.

That night they went to bed early.

Outside, the worm in the yard wriggled to the grate and then wriggled back again, crossing and re-crossing the cold tiles. The wind sharpened in the night. Water seeped into the heel-marks on the waste ground and a frost spread slowly over the fields and the streets. It stiffened the grass and formed thin ice in all the holes. It crawled over the dead leaves under the palings and veined them white. Under the goal-post stones it crept and the creepers bored away from it. It froze the breadcrumbs to the ground and hardened a rag that floated in a puddle. Now it had covered the fields, freezing every little pond and the hoof-marks of horses, and now it was spreading on the roof-tops and dusting every stone and every tree. The worm lay still and a thin flake of ice froze it to the tiles.

In the early morning the alarm clock rang and the mother stopped it before it should waken Clare.

Colm got out of bed on to the cold floor when she shook

him by the shoulder. The air in the room was thin and cold. The waste ground was white and the sky blue-black. From the window he saw frost on the clothes-peg on the line and on the holly in the corner. It was a lovely Christmas morning. The bells of the Monastery were ringing loudly.

The streets were silent and the frost sparkled under the lamp light. Here and there he could hear a door closing and see firelight leaping against the window panes.

He went to St Paul's. The chapel lights were lit and the hot pipes gave out a golden glow of heat. In one corner shone a cave of light from the Crib and across the High Altar were snowy letters suspended by invisible threads – GLORIA IN EXCELSIS DEO.

It was all quiet and strange so early in the morning. People were moving up to the altar rails to receive Holy Communion: women with shawls, old men with sticks, and he saw the manager of the bakery and his two sons walking in front with heads lowered and hands joined.

Colm felt very happy; he would wait till the end of Mass before receiving Holy Communion. A priest came out in white vestments. A bell rang and the Sacrifice began. Colm followed the words in his missal, and at the Consecration he closed his book and bowed his head in adoration, and said a prayer he had learned in the Religious Instruction class in the College:

> *Into the chalice of the Mass that is being offered up I place my father's soul and Alec's soul and the souls of all my friends and relations. Cleanse them, O Christ, from all stain of sin with one drop of your precious blood* ... And he raised his eyes to the uplifted chalice: *My Lord and my God, I adore Thee.*

He felt cleansed; and after receiving the Blessed Eucharist he visited the Crib and mentally compared its rich elaboration with Jamesy's little box of straw.

When he came out of the church the sky was losing its darkness. The houses were cold under their frosted slates and many windows were lighted. He heard children blowing bugles in their bedrooms and others shouting: 'Look what I got! Look what Daddy Christmas brought me!'

A woman stood at an open door cleaning a pair of shoes in the dim light from the sky. Lighted candles shone in some windows and tinsel glittered on Christmas trees.

As he turned the corner of his own street he noticed wheel-marks in the frost and saw a taxi outside the door. He ran into the house and there in the kitchen was Joe, Theresa, and the baby wrapped in a blanket. They had crossed that morning to spend the Christmas at home.

Colm ran up the stairs to waken Jamesy. He got up at once and placed the crib on the trunk and lit the lamp. Clare was sitting up in bed rummaging through the contents of her stocking. As Jamesy carried her out to see the crib Theresa was coming upstairs with the baby and when Clare saw her she shouted with delight and turned away from the crib: 'Ah, Theresa, let me nurse her! Let me nurse her!'

Clare jumped back to bed again and Theresa put the baby beside her and propped two pillows and two chairs alongside the bed. The baby gripped the celluloid doll and ground her teeth in its head.

Down stairs there was great chatter and the smell of frying bacon. They were all talking at once: Theresa about her home in Birmingham and the new curtains that she had got: Joe about his work and the football matches; and Jamesy mimicking old McGrath when he was sacking him.

'What about coming to Birmingham as an apprentice?' Joe suggested, half in fun.

'Would you like that?' the mother asked, at the same time winking at Joe.

'Man, I'd go now!' Jamesy enthused.

And so they talked, the jest becoming earnest, until it was finally decided that Jamesy would go back with them. And when Mrs Heaney came in and heard it she put her hand to her breast and exclaimed: 'Now, now, I never heard the like of that. There's nothing like a trade, Mary. A man with a trade is a man with money in his pocket. Now, what's a shop-boy? – Once he's out of work he has nothing and can do nothing. But a trade, Mary – there's nothing to beat a trade. And Jamesy can come home in five years' time and snap his fingers at McGrath and his potato-weighing.'

But for Colm a sadness hung over the whole day when he heard Jamesy talking about the things he would take away with him.

In the evening they were all gathered in the kitchen and the baby was asleep in Clare's bed. They laughed and joked, but all the time everyone was conscious of Alec, trying not to speak of him.

Colm was asked to sing, but he said that he had a sore throat.

Mrs Heaney turned to Jamesy: 'Now, Jamesy, you'll give us the 'Turf Man'; God knows when we'll hear it again!'

With great bluster Jamesy stood out in the floor and commenced his song. But when he had finished he struck his chest with his right hand, an action of Alec's, and the mother noticed it and fell silent, and as they clapped she went into the scullery and pretended to work around the sink.

The morning came. Jamesy pulled out old waist-coats from the chest of drawers. He came across a card with a fretwork saw attached to it. He began to pack.

'Do you know, Colm,' he was saying, 'when I get to Birmingham I'm going to invent a great rabbit hutch that'll keep out draughts, and someday you'll see my name in the paper.'

Colm only nodded.

In the early afternoon when he saw Theresa putting Jamesy's old clothes into her case he went out. He took a tram and got off when it reached the end of the lines. He was in open country. The air was clear and cold, the hedges black and ragged and the bare thorns glistening with drops of melted frost. The road was black and to his right snow lay in the crevices of the mountain. He walked aimlessly, not caring, and then he came to the Lagan and turned along the tow-path.

An exhausted wintry sun was setting in amber behind him. The river flowed black and still, carrying a flock of clouds upon its back. At one place bubbles came to the surface, broke and made little circles on the water; some eel, he thought, foraging in the mud below.

A chill mist rose from the ground. Two men passed with greyhounds on leads. Swans with wings akimbo were moving up to the quieter reaches for the night, a fan of wavelets widening behind them. No birds were singing. The waterfall lumbered into a pool and wrinkles of froth with groups of bubbles came and broke in the eddies. The grass on the banks was combed by the water. The fields were deserted and their grass limp and grey.

And all this beauty, all these quiet places flowed into his heart and filled him with a tired-torn joy. And turning out of it he came to the city and the lights of the tram at the end of the road. The conductor and driver were smoking within. Everything was quiet. But as the tram moved off towards the centre of the city, down from the big houses to the long narrow streets, a vague fear came over him, fear of shots ringing out and splintering the glass. The tram raced on almost empty. It lit up the houses at each side of the road, and once he glimpsed, in the fanlight of a house, a ship in a bottle, and recalled the thundery day that he had taken his leave of Uncle Robert.

In the kitchen they were at their tea when he came in. Two suit-cases stood on the floor. The baby was crying.

Colm went down to the boat to see them go away. Coming back it was very cold; there would be frost tonight again. He put his hand in the letter-box and caught the string attached to the lock. He let himself in. The light was out in the kitchen and his mother was sitting at a sunken fire. Her prayer beads and a comb were on the table. He told her that everything went off all right and he passed out into the yard. He stood at the open back-door looking out on the dark waste ground. A police 'cage' raced up the hill beyond the palings. He came inside and bolted the door.

He went up to bed, and on the landing saw the lamp burning before the crib and above it a wavering circle of light on the ceiling. In bed he lay awake, his mind swirling to and fro . . . rabbits wild and free on the hills around Belfast . . . swans moving across black water . . . oil-lamps warming the windows in Rathlin . . . a rusty tin in the fork of a thorn bush . . . a rickle of bones falling dead in York Street . . .

MICHAEL McLAVERTY
Collected
Short Stories

Edited with an afterword by
SOPHIA HILLAN

Introduction by
SEAMUS HEANEY

MICHAEL McLAVERTY, one of Ireland's most distinguished short story writers, painted with acute precision and intensity the northern landscapes of his homeland – lonely hill farms, rough island terrain and the tight backstreets of Belfast. Focusing on moments of passion, wonder or bitter disenchantment in lives that are a continuous struggle towards the light, these stories, in the compassion of the tone and the spare purity of the language, are nothing short of masterly.

Beautifully illustrated with specially commissioned wood engravings by Barbara Childs, and including an introduction by Seamus Heaney and an afterword by editor Sophia Hillan, this handsome edition is a fitting celebration of a writer who has been compared to Chekhov and Joyce.

ISBN 0 85640 727 5
£14.99